Not Far From Town

Also by Brian A. Connolly

Bradley's Christmas Adventure
Wolf Journal

Not Far From Town

Stories from the Upper Allegheny River

By Brian A. Connolly

Virtualbookworm.com Publishing
College Station, Texas

Several of the stories in this collection have appeared in other publications: *Portage Creek* in Indigenous Fiction, Redmond, Washington; *Turtle Point* in Ibis Review, Falls Village, Connecticut; *Lillibridge Creek* in Potato Eyes Magazine, Troy, Maine.

Cover Photograph: Soda Butte Creek, copyright 2006 by Dan and Cindy Hartman. Used by permission. Courtesy of Wildlife Along the Rockies, Silver Gate, Montana.
www.wildlifealongtherockies.homestead.com.

Author Photograph by Heather Jerome

This collection of stories is a work of fiction. The characters and events are products of the author's imagination. Any similarity to real people and events is coincidental.

"Not Far From Town" by Brian A. Connolly. ISBN 1-58939-865-3 (softcover).

Library of Congress Control Number: 2006926159

For
Mike, Mary Ann, Judy, Kathy, Kate,
Chris and Jani

Acknowledgements

Special thanks to Kevin Porter, a member of the International Society of Professional Trackers and NYS DEC Certified Search and Rescue Crew Boss from Cato, New York, who taught me about foraging in the wild and about the art of tanning hides. Also, special thanks to R. Edson Porter of Auburn, New York, for his *Kinzua* insights. Thanks to Bob Wiltermood, Port Orchard, Washington, for his expertise in firearms. Thank you to the Potter County Historical Society in Coudersport, Pennsylvania (the town where I was born) for their detailed information and photos of the hamlet of Mina, Pennsylvania. Thank you, as well, to Robert Adam, Fishkill, New York, for his gentle encouragement, and his phonographic memory of '60's music. Thank you to Judy Connolly for her computer wisdom!

Author's Note

The novella *Mina* evolved from the short story *Bear Creek*.
Both locations are not far from Port Allegany, Pennsylvania.
Most of the stories in this collection happen in real places just
upstream or downstream from Port. When I knew that the novella
would end in Mina, I decided to check my memory against the
facts, whatever they were. What I knew was that back in the '50's
my mother used to take my brothers, sisters, and me to this 'ghost
town' she called Mina. It was across the Allegheny River
between Roulette and Coudersport. She would walk us among the
scant ruins of this turn of the century hamlet. What remained of
the once busy lumber town were vine covered foundations,
partial windowless walls, broken clapboards burnt brown with
age, and a few remnant fireplaces made of gray stone. Our
imaginations rebuilt the town with the aid of my mother's stories.
Just to make sure that what I remembered was somewhat
accurate, I contacted the Potter County Historical Society in
Coudersport, Pennsylvania. They assured me that all traces of
Mina had been washed away during the great flood of 1942,
many years before I visited the 'ghost town'. I didn't understand
how my memory could be so faulty. As a consolation, the
historical society member with whom I spoke, said he'd send me
some photographs and an article on Mina from their files. Some
of the photographs sent to me were part of a multi-page
newspaper article titled *The History of Mina* by Alyce Hoh
Connolly, my mother. So the clear details of the Mina in my
memory were actually the details of the Mina from my mother's
memory. Maybe my story telling springs from the same well. The
dilemma was that my story takes place in recent time and ends in
a town that no longer exists. I decided as a tribute to her, I would
allow the story to end in the 'ghost town' of our imagination. I
am sure she would have approved.

Not Far From Town

Stories from the Upper Allegheny River
by
Brian A. Connolly

Table of Contents

Kinzua

Sebastian Baxter was like a character from one of the novels I was studying at Edinboro College. I met him in Garland, a one street town west of the Allegheny National Forest in northern Pennsylvania. It was two a. m. when he stopped to offer me a ride.

"How far ya goin', partner?" he asked.

"Port Allegany," I said.

"Get in then. We'll get you down the road a piece. This is a hell of a place to get stuck in. No women, no booze, no women. Just old farty maids. Makes a man uncomftable just to look at 'em. I can get ya to Ormsby. No women there either, but at least there's a light an' trucks commin' through. You won't be far from home then. Hell, you could walk from there!"

I threw my duffle bag in the back seat and rode shotgun. Sebastian was driving a '54 Ford wagon that must have doubled as a farm vehicle. No hubcaps, rear passenger door tied shut with bailing twine and the car's original sky blue paint was clouded with rust. The hood was sprung, and, even though it wasn't raining, I noticed that he only had a windshield wiper on his side. There was a hole in the muffler causing it to sound like war drums. The car smelled of chickens and hay, and Sebastian smelled of wood smoke. On the

1

crackling AM radio, Marty Robins was singing about his Mexican girl down in El Paso.

Sebastian was a big man. Not tall, but chunky with a great belly which was covered with a stained, gray flannel shirt and protruded through dingy red suspenders. He wore old blue work pants like the kind the factory workers back home wear. Locks of long, gray hair dangled from under his colorless felt hat. His face was round, red from a life outdoors, shored up with a double chin that was softened by a five-day white stubble. His face was alive and excited as if he were pleased to see me. Even by the dash lights I could see the yellow discoloration of his fingers from years of smoking Luckys. He offered me one. I accepted.

We headed down the narrow macadam road to Route 6, then east toward the lights of Warren. It was a clear, fall night. Stars hung above the dark trees, strings of costume jewelry: bracelets, necklaces, earrings and brooches laid out on black cloth as if they were the real thing.

"The name's Sebastian, Sebastian Baxter of the Ormsby Baxters!" he said.

"Jonathan Cole," I said shaking his hand. My hand was soft; his was hard, callused and dry. A firm grip.

"Where ya hitchin' from?"

"Edinboro. I'm in my second year at the college there," I said.

Sebastian said, "Gonna be a professor, I bet! It's a good thing yer doin'. Book learnin' weren't my strong suit. God knows I had some brave teachers who tried, but it was all water agin stone. I can read and write some, but on the farm there ain't much call fer it. Made it through the eighth grade though! Well, not all the way through. But they's other kinds of learnin'. For example, I know the woods and can read a trail as good as any guide in these here hills. Get my deer and a bear most every year along with a flock of turkeys, grouse and geese!

"And then there's the farm. What a education that's been. But I do all right. Made it to sixty-three and the good Lord hasn't seen fit to drop a boulder on me yet!"

"Sounds like a hard life," I said.

"All life is hard no matter who you are: farmer, professor or president," Sebastian said. "Life is trouble. The trick is to squeeze enough fun out of it to make the rest tolerable. If there's excitement around, I'll go fer it. Never miss a chance! So that way I'm fortified fer bad times like when the old wife died a few years back, and just last week my cow keeled over dead as if she was shot, and the tractor's broke good. What kin ya do? Ya got to keep yer balance. I seen guys go off their nut in bad times. Yellin' at the sky in a rage! Don't do no good. I tried it. So, do they teach that at yer college?"

"What?" I said.

"How to keep yer balance," he said.

"I think they expect you to figure that out on your own."

Sebastian lit another Lucky and said, "Well, you got a good start on it. Standing out here in the middle of the planet at two o'clock in the dark a.m. Gives a man a chance to think about things. And not just 'Am I going to be jumped by a bear?', but like 'Am I doin' the right thing with my life?', 'Do I like who I am?' That sort of stuff. There's somethin' I wanna show you up the road just the other side of Warren. We'll take old 59 to Ormsby. It'll save us time, and I kin show you what real hardship looks like. It'll be part of yer education, professor!"

The lights of Warren were like an island in the middle of a dark sea. Patsy Cline was falling to pieces on the radio. There was an aunt of mine on my father's side who lived here. Still did as far as I knew. I told Sebastian about her, "She has a big house a few blocks off Main Street somewhere, and collects newspapers and magazines, especially The National Geographic. I think she had every issue they published. Her house was so full of stacks and stacks that you could only walk narrow paths from room to room. I always thought she was a little touched, but dad said she had read them all and that they were carefully arranged by year. He said she called it her private library. She had never been anywhere, but she could tell you all about the head hunting tribes of New Guinea or about the rituals of the Inuit people in the Arctic."

"Sounds like my kind a' woman!" Sebastian said. "You see, I'm a collector myself. Mostly busted farm machinery. I got me a steam tractor though, hand built by Foster there in Smethport back in eighteen and ninety-five. I refitted it, and she works slick as lace on a young girl's bottom. Still use it fer spring plowin'. Even had her over to the McKean County Fair last year.

"Also, I collects Indian relics. Got a whole slew of arrowheads, stone axes and such stuff. Seneca mostly, but some is Susquehannock and Huron. Found it all just plowin' my fields. Them Indians was good people until we run 'em off or kilt 'em outright. They knew how to be with the land.

"So, the old aunt is a collector! What say we give her a visit!"

"I think it's a little late, Sebastian, and I'm not exactly sure which house is hers," I said.

"Next time then," he said. "Besides, we got something of our own up ahead."

Sebastian pulled a disk shaped box of Skoal out of his shirt pocket, took a large pinch and packed it behind his lower lip. "Have some?" he mumbled.

"Oh, no thanks," I said.

"Could you take the lid offen that Maxwell can there by yer leg?" he asked.

A putrid smell sprung from the can as I removed the lid. Inside sloshed the inky remains of spent tobacco juice. I held back a gag and placed the open can on the floor hump between us. Sebastian spit out a long, dark string of liquid toward my foot. It arched into the open can.

"Pretty damn good shot, ain't I?" he said.

"Yes," I said.

"When yer a growed man," he continued, "you'll learn yerself the pleasures of a good pinch a' tobacca. Nothin' like it!"

"My father's first paying job," I explained, "was cleaning the spittoons at the Butler House in Port. He was twelve."

"He must be a good man with such a good start as that!" Sebastian smiled.

Sebastian settled into driving and thinking. The lights of Warren were absorbed by the dark hills behind us as we headed east on Route 59. The headlights searched the macadam road like luminous antennae, and Woody Guthrie sang on the radio about hoboes riding the rails. I watched the trees and the starry sky and occasionally glimpsed the Allegheny River running dark and cold through the endless mountain shadows. As we moved along the winding road, I remembered something my father used to say: Life isn't just what happens when you arrive some place. Most of it happens along the way there. So true, I thought. So true.

We rounded a sharp curve and descended into a thickly forested valley. A half dozen deer were standing in the road. Sebastian honked at them and shouted out the window, "Just you wait! Your life's gonna change soon!"

"What do you mean by that?" I asked.

"You'll see up ahead about a mile or so," he smiled. "Everyone's life here is gonna change. In fact, professor, you an' me might be the very last people to ride this road!"

The first evidence of change came at a roadside rest where several yellow bulldozers and a giant grader were parked. A little way down the road the forest stopped. All the trees were gone. The hillside was barren, all neatly graded as far up as I could see. Fresh earth smells streamed into the car window. Down by the river concrete footings had been poured; the forms were still in place, and re-bars protruded above. Several spotlights attached to cranes illuminated the area. Men with kerosene lanterns stood in small groups on both sides of the water. Small campfires dotted the shoreline with their dancing light.

"What's going on here?" I asked.

"It's the Kinzua Dam they're building. They say it's a flood protection project. Those men over there are guards. They expect trouble. Some people don't think a dam should be built, especially the ones whose land is going to be under a hundred feet of water. You see, this here is reservation land, Indian land. It belongs to Cornplanter's people. They're Seneca. The land was give to them in the 1800's , how did they say, 'as long as the grass growed and the river flows'. Well, the govement got rid of the grass problem by removing it all, just like skinnin' a bear, but the river's still flowin'. They'll stop that soon enough. And these good people are offen their land."

"Judas priest," I said, "look at this place!"

Sebastian said, "Just wait 'til ya see what's up ahead. We're just a spit away from what's left of the village of Kinzua, a Seneca town."

This part of the road was very rough having broken under the weight of heavy equipment: skidders, eighteen-wheelers and such. Ahead was a grove of trees. All the branches had been severed. The dismembered trunks stood like lifeless ghosts, sorrowfully still, dishonored in their death.

Sebastian drove beyond the trees before he pulled over to the side of the road. Up a slight embankment was a ten-foot high wall of black plastic above which shown the bright haze of hidden lights.

"This is what I want you to see. You'll remember tonight! Come on," he said.

We left the car idling and both doors open. Over the low thunder of the muffler, Tennessee Ernie Ford could be heard singing *Sixteen Tons*. Sebastian led me up to the black wall. There were dozens of tear holes scattered along its length where people had cut through to see what was on the other side. Through each hole a crisp shaft of light jabbed the cool darkness. I could hear voices.

"Have yerself a look see," Sebastian said.

I peered through the nearest hole. At first my eye had to adjust to the silver lights. The area inside was glowing with bulbs strung from poles and kerosene lanterns carried by the men inside. There must have been over thirty men working. The eerie thing was that each man was dressed in white coveralls, white gloves and black rubber boots. Each one wore a white hood with netting over the face. The hoods were fastened to the white suits. Strapped to their heads were miner's lights. Some of the men were digging with shovels, others with picks. Still others were carrying long boxes or black bags on stretchers. Mostly I couldn't make out what they were saying, but one man nearest me yelled, "I got me a live one here and there's no goddamn box! Al, get me one of them bags!"

It was as if I had stumbled onto men working on another planet. Without turning away from the scene, I asked Sebastian what they were doing.

"This here's the village burial ground. These men are digging up graves to transplant them to the new burial ground up in New York. Quite a sight isn't it! They wear the suits to keep from getting some disease. One guy told me last week that when the job is done, these guys have to be quarantined for three to six months. But the pay is good! Can't blame a guy for makin' a livin'. I think the only sickness they is likely to get is soul sickness, haunted by what they seen and done, not to mention the Indian spirits followin' 'em around the rest of their days. The tribes here abouts knows how to put on a good spell and there ain't no escaping it.

"Can you imagine how Cornplanter's people feels what with their parents being dug up, their sisters and brothers being dug up, their children and the old ones being hauled out the ground. Why if the gov'ment came to dig up my old wife, rest her soul, I'd sit on her grave with that bear gun a' mine and help them fellas to join her ifn they didn't leave her be!

"See that black ridge up yonder where the stars end? I bet a gang of pissed off Senecas is up there right now crouched in the dark wearin' war paint, armed to the teeth. And I don't blame 'em one goddamn bit! You reads history about the Indian wars a hundred year ago and all the terrible things we did to them so we could have a free land and they could just be lost in their own land, but the same damn thing is still goin' on! The gov'ment makes a decision and everything agin it is just fleas on a dog.

"Professor, what yer lookin' at through that hole is called progress. This here is the real face of progress not some mask the newspapers 'r history books wants ya to see. They's all full a' lies an' cover-ups! They only show you what we build. They forgets to mention all the things we destroyed. The trees, the people, the land, the animals. Makes no difference to them bastards! What matters to them is a hundred miles a' shoreline for swimming an' boating, electric power and control over this here river what's been runnin' its own wild way long since before even the Indian was here.

"I think we better go before I decides to join them Indians on the ridge. I didn't mean to get so riled, but I just don't understand it, I don't understand how people can do what they do to other people. Assholes! That's what they are!"

Sebastian was still mumbling to himself as he ambled down the slope to the car. We drove on in silence into the village of Kinzua.

There were more tree trunks standing armless. Oaks and maples mostly. It was spooky driving through the empty streets. Except for three old, boarded up houses and a stone church, everything else had been bulldozed and carried away.

Sebastian pointed to a vacant corner lot. "There was a combination post office, store, hotel and tavern right there. And over there was a hardware and smith shop. The brothers that run it could fix anything that broke, make up new harness and shoe a horse after they made the shoes. They fixed my bear gun when the damn pin busted.

"The gov'ment will take those last three houses down, but they's some talk of leavin' the church be. After all, the water will be eighty feet deep here inside a year. Bass and muskellunge will be prayin' in it."

The whole town was recreated out of Sebastian's memory. The old people sitting on stoops in the late afternoon sun. Children singing in the schoolhouse. Young women weaving in their living rooms or working in gardens. Men farming the flats along the river.

"You see, professor," Sebastian said, "what the damn gov'ment don't understand is that everythin' I just told you was also bulldozed and carried away. All the feelin's those people had, their own history here all plowed under. Now I ain't Indian, not a drop, but the old wife, she was half Seneca. These was her people. And I knowd them all. Now they's all moved up to New York. Gov'ment says 'we'll gives you a new piece of land and a brand new trailer and all these folks had to do was give up their life. It's just a damn shame is what it is! A damn shame!"

Sebastian didn't talk much after that. He was lost in his own history, brooding about the 'gov'ment'. We moved through the dark mountains along Route 59 passing through Marshburg, Laffayette and Mt. Alton. The radio played broken dream songs.

We arrived at the blinking light in Ormsby just as daylight was beginning to stain the eastern sky. Sebastian pulled over and said, "This is where you get out, professor. My farm's just up toward Cyclone a ways. You'll have the sun to keep you company shortly, and in no time at all them logging trucks'll come through n' give ya a ride. What I'd like ya to do fer me is when you get back to that college of yours, remember what you saw tonight. Just remember."

I shook Sebastian's hand and thanked him for the ride. I promised him I would remember. He pulled out onto the road, his muffler drumming out a warning to the neighboring tribes. Hank William's *I'm So Lonesome I Could Die* trailed Sebastian as he headed north. I stood next to my duffle bag looking down the empty road. The silence was immense. No ride was in sight. The caution light blinked on and off, on and off, making the yellow crossroads appear and disappear, appear and disappear.

Portage Creek

She moved along the creek bank silent as a deer. The fish were not disturbed; they were used to her the way they were used to the diamond light flashing on the surface. The early morning light flooded this section of the woods through which the creek struggled, constricted. She was humming to herself, to the birds, the trees. She wore a dandelion in her hair. The rush of the water took over her thinking, massaged the stories she told herself the way water caresses stones until the frivolous is smoothed away and just the hard truth remains.

The town's people said that she lived on Portage Creek her whole life, forty years of water. Born in the cottage, raised on trout, married there and, when everyone died off like fall grass, lived on alone. Her kin were all lost to the sickness, even the boy. She was spared. This was one of the stories she told herself. After all the details were gotten through, guilt was what remained. Why her? Why not let the youngest live, oh please, God, take me, she had said over twenty years ago. Another prayer unanswered.

She stopped at the creek bend where the deeper water swirled gray-black in eddies that moved out from the cut bank, grew in strength and died in the rapids. She leaned over the water staring at her reflection. A wrinkled face looked back. This is how she saw herself, not how she was. Her long, brown hair, the color of late summer wheat, trailed like willow branches in the water. She kissed the water. Below the surface, smooth, gray stones and drowned logs looked up.

She undid the shell buttons of her dress, and the floral print fell in a heap among the ferns at her feet. Light bathed her body. She wore its warmth like a cloak. Now she was an animal from the forest come to bathe. The moving water slid over her skin, a cool, silk gown. Her breasts were alert under the flowing water. She could feel the energy rising in her like sap moving in the veins of a tree. She lay with her feet pointing downstream in the sweet water, inhaling its mossy fragrance before submerging herself completely. She looked like a snag, a sunken birch around which the water danced and made its signature and erased it many times.

There are those in the village who say she becomes a fish, a brown trout that hides in a hollow under the bank until intruders leave. One fisherman said he found her there, submerged and naked, her arms dangling in the current. He knew she was dead. He put down his rod and creel, and, when he looked back, she was gone. A brown trout was moving up through the rapids. Another, older man, said she knew the secrets of deer, of coyote and that she understood the sorrow of flowers.

She rose up out of the creek and dried herself on the pebble beach. She thought of what her father often said. Some people are fishermen, some are fish and others are bait. She thought about the bait people, innocent, terrified, tied to the hook or pierced and dangling, numb with grief. Sometimes she thought of herself as one of those people.

Her way to survive was the daily baptism that washed away like old skin, the broken dream of her life. Nature is cruel and beautiful, she thought. She pulled on her dress and moved like a deer downstream toward the cottage. In the deep water of the creek, the brown trout, suspended in mossy light, whispered quietly to each other.

Turtle Point

Harry walked slowly through the stubble of cornfield. The furrows were straight, but the ground was irregular and difficult to read in the dark. He was careful to keep the barrel of the twelve gauge pointed at the sky. It was three a. m. When he looked back, he could see the porch light he had left on. From this distance, it looked like the torch of a tiny star.

Dried cornstalks crunched under Harry's boots. The air tasted as though it might snow soon. At his approach, a dozen deer bounded off toward the river woods where he was headed. The thud of their hooves jolted the dark silence. Then the quiet rushed in and smothered the intruding noise the way water flows back when it has been pushed away. Harry continued.

This had been McAdam's field. Old Man McAdam had been mean all his life. Posted his land and shot at people who trespassed. He never hit anyone, but his point was well made. Harry thought about last summer when the old man got drunk, fell off his Alice Chalmers and slid under the disk harrow. At the wake down in Port, people said a lot of nice things about McAdam none of which was true. Harry had been his neighbor twenty years and had never talked to him except over a gun barrel. Some said that losing that eye to a bear made him mean, but Harry felt it went back further than that.

Where the stars were missing up ahead, Harry could sense the outline of the woods. What am I doing here? he thought to himself. He hadn't slept for nights. Something was wrong, but he couldn't say what it was. His feet tangled in a rooted stalk, and he pitched forward onto the ground. The gun did not go off. The earth was wet, nearly frozen, but still gave off its worm smell. Harry lay there for a moment, the weight of the stars pressing down on his back. He raised himself to his knees, scraped mud off his hands and the gun barrel. He worked the pump ejecting three red Winchester pumpkin ball slugs. Those he placed in the pocket of the vest he wore under his canvas coat. He checked the muzzle with his thumb to make certain that it was not plugged. Harry stood, pulled his gloves from the game pocket in the back of his coat and went on more carefully toward the woods.

He found the abandoned logging road that cut through the woods to the river. Brush had grown up. Leafless sticks scratched the canvas coat. The scent of pine, oak, shagbark hickory, leaf duff and ground mold perfumed the woods. Harry felt comfortable and moved as naturally as the deer along this dark scar of a road.

The river was closer than Harry had remembered. It, too, had a smell, the odor of memory, damp decay, a living soup. The bank was high on this side. It was equally high on the other side, but could not be seen in the dark. The stars floated on the deep water of the Allegheny like a swarm of glowing bugs, alive and nervous. Harry hesitated in the dark and listened. The river slid along the narrow bend, muttered some, but mostly, Harry thought, sounded like the slithering of a large snake whose scales slip along the muddy bottom, and those dark, penetrating eyes and, oh, that awful tongue. Harry admired the river. He loved the way it had direction and limits. The way it flowed. It moved along the curve of the earth, and the lesser streams flowed into it, tumbled down the mountains, cut through the valley in a rush to join the river. Lillibridge, Skinner, Portage, Coombs creeks and streams with no names gave the river their strength, nourished the river.

Upstream the bank was low. This is where the animals came to drink. Harry had seen raccoon, otter, 'possum, coyote and a young bear here at different times. But mostly the run through the woods that led here was worn by deer. Harry remembered the last time that he was here was late afternoon in the fall twenty years ago. He had startled a Great Blue heron who lifted out of the water with great flaps of gray-blue wings as if it were a piece of the sky rising through the autumn blaze, water dripping from its long legs. He recalled being happy for weeks after that single moment's encounter.

Near the deer run where the ground swelled, Harry picked a spot to wait. A great oak rose like a pillar holding up the dark. Harry stood with his back against the rough bark and reloaded the gun. For a long time he stood silently looking in the direction the deer would come. Hours passed, days passed, years went by. Daylight was still an hour away.

New stars had moved in to take the place of ones who had moved on. Once upon a time long ago, Harry had given the constellations his own personal names because he could not understand the names others had given them. Arrowhead, the Kite, Sleeping Coyote, Fallen Tree, River of Stars, and Owl Eyes were some of the names he remembered now. One day, he thought, I'll write them down. Maybe it will help.

As other thoughts came to him, he weighed their importance. Some he cast off. Others he allowed to linger. He threw out people he had lost. Parents gone. Wife and child lost in the fire. They were old scars now. No use summoning ghosts. He decided, too, not to think about outside troubles like the job at the glass plant, the leak in the kitchen roof, the busted car.

Harry focused on something he hadn't allowed himself to think about for a long time. He hid it from himself, kept it buried in a locked drawer deep inside. He had hoped it would go away, dry up, but it was only waiting for him the way he was waiting for the deer. Harry knew now why he had come here in the middle of the night. He shuddered and waited. His eyes strained to see what was out in the dark woods. He saw nothing but the trunks of trees huddled together.

Harry thought about emptiness, feeling hollow, unable to feel as if the wires of emotion were all down. Everything was dammed up, held back, contained. For a long time he had felt the pressure building. Harry thought to himself that he had no idea when this began. He remembered laughter and crying and hope and longing and sorrow and happiness that seemed to have no source. He remembered the heron, the joy of seeing it as if it were a gift.

Deep in the woods branches snapped. Harry shouldered his shotgun and clicked off the safety. Even though he hadn't hunted in years, these movements were automatic. A smudge of daylight had entered the woods. The leafless branches were fine ink drawings against the pearl of the eastern sky. Harry waited. He calmed his breathing. The deer moved along the run like the minute hand on a clock. Harry watched as they stepped and browsed, stepped and browsed some more. What there was of wind came off the river over the run toward Harry. The deer could detect no human scent. He, however, could smell them. Musk permeated the half dark like an invisible smoke. Somewhere close, a buck was in rut. The yearlings passed first followed by a half dozen doe. Harry allowed each one to step into his sights, then out. He waited. His arms ached. He was afraid to lower the gun though. They would see him and bolt away. He held steady.

When the buck appeared on the path, Harry gasped. The animal was immense. Harry estimated that it would field dress at two hundred pounds. Its antlers were magnificent...thick as wrists at the base, bone curving up and out a full two feet with a half dozen spikes each. Harry's heart thumped. To shoot now would be like shooting the heron. He lowered the barrel of the shotgun. Although the deer could not see Harry, it now knew that he was there, and it looked right at him. The buck lowered his head and jerked it up to see if Harry would move again. Harry was stone. The animal stomped the ground and snorted great puffs of air. Harry did not move.

Finally, the deer vanished. No sound of crashing branches or hooves splashing in the river. Just silence. Harry ejected the shells from the gun and slid them into his pocket. He squatted next to the tree with his head buried in his arms. He could feel it coming from deep within. The dam had been blown up. The river was free again and flowing. A wall of water rushed down the valley soaking the dry, cracked earth; filling the empty streambed with its silvery light; tumbling wet over parched stones and dead wood. Dusty roots drank the water and swelled; wildflowers lifted their heads; fish leapt in the tumultuous current and herons glided above like pieces of sky coming to feed at the river. For joy and sorrow, Harry sobbed. For all the moments he had erased from his heart, he cried aloud. For the moving river, he wept.

Skinner Creek

Words are sometimes hard to come by which is strange because they are so plentiful. The feelings were very real, ever-present, deep rooted, rose through the body like a tide, but he had trouble when it came to naming those feelings. The old man said to me, "What I'm afraid of is that the very saying of it might cause it to die. It's like the words themselves will take the power of it from me. I've been not wanting to say it cuz some feelings is like birds, they just need the sky, the woods, the creek to live in. To stuff 'em up with words is to lock 'em in a cage. They may seem perty to look at for a while, but what you don't see about a caged bird is its sadness like a hidden stone. So the words are there for the saying all right. I just ain't been willin' to line 'em up in a certain way as to hold in such a small space a thing as immense as the feeling I have for this old crick. I could weep right now here in front of you and that, my boy, would be as clear an expression of my relationship to Skinner Crick as any organized bunch of words. Don't worry yourself none. I'll try to keep aholt of myself."

The old man and I were fishing the creek with worms and having no luck, which was the reason he got to talking. The rule was that talking and fishing don't mix. The reason wasn't because it would scare the fish but that fishing was thinking time. The old man had said, "Just let the gurgling flow of the water and the changing light wash over ya and yer thinkin' will be as clear as the hill spring. There's more to fishin' than just fish! It's the silence part of it that helps us figure out all the mess we're in when we're away from the crick."

His name was Corbin. For years he taught me about fishing and hunting. When fishing a cove along the Allegheny, if a turtle is around, grab him and tie him by a hind leg to a tree so's he can't go in the water and warn the fishes. To the old man, the turtle was the messenger between two worlds. Of course, if the turtle happened to be a snapper the size of a hubcap, we'd haul him home. The old man would get that ugly head (he called it beautiful) to clamp onto a broken broom handle. I can still feel the sound of the axe taking the head off and feel the blood splatter on our faces and see the head still holding tight on that stick, its eyes kind of with a surprised look on them. Quick as skinning a bullhead, he would axe open the shell, toss the guts on the ground for the barn cats and dice the turtle into chunks. The chowder he made had cream from the top of the milk pail, potatoes, peas, a few carrots, mushrooms we'd collected up on Sleeping Bear, a pile of onions or leeks, if we had them. Cook it all together about half a day. It was a feast! Before we ate he always paid his respects to the turtle thanking it for giving itself to us, and saying he hoped we were worthy to receive such a fine turtle.

Another specialty of his was raccoon stew. He kept a bunch of coon hounds for hunting and trained the young hounds with a German shepherd. The old man told me, "It's natural for these hounds to chase a coon for half the night if need be to tree 'em, but once the coon is treed, them dogs don't know enough to bark. The shepherd'll bark his head off teaching the others what to do."

But it was fishing we were concerned with or rather talking or rather him talking and me listening. "To say it right out," he continued while fingering his line, "this crick with its twists and bends, deep holes and rapids, sandbars and cut banks is Milly. She was such a sweet one, a good wife, a real companion. You didn't know her cuz of her being gone before you was born. Twenty-two years now she's gone. There wasn't a thing she loved more 'n just being with the crick or in it or watchin' it from up in them woods. She didn't have much use for the town or the people in it. Not that there was a thing wrong with 'em. They looked on her as strange, which she was. When different ones would come out to the farm to fetch milk or potatoes or corn, they'd see her sittin' on the bank starin' into the water. She'd still be there when they left. Peculiar was the word they used.

"But for Milly it weren't a bit peculiar. She could talk even better 'n me and was book learned to boot! She always said the town's people were too busy to know real livin'. Her 'meditations' as she called 'em was a kind of religion, a spiritual thing. She'd lived her whole life in this valley with no hankerin' to go anywheres else. She'd say so many was restless cuz they didn't know the place they was in and hoped to find what they needed to fill an emptiness somewheres else. Milly never felt the emptiness. She said the only thing that made her feel lonely was being indoors. She was like this wild thing spending her days tryin' to throw off any tame that was in her. She had read on her own long before I come along a guy name of Muir and that Burroughs fella and the poet Whitman and the one whose name always slips me who lived at the pond. Milly said they was ones that 'listened to the earth and felt its life move, heard its heart beating.' Sounds a bit crazy, I admit. I even thought as much when we first met. Before she'd agree to marry, she said I had to understand how she was and not always be tryin' to change her into something else. I always tried to accept folks for who they was, but it took some time to really know Milly.

"She'd disappear into the woods for hours on end, sometimes in the middle of the night without a light. Often I'd find her just at first light sittin' by this very pool talkin' out loud as if she was with her very best friend, but no one was about. She was talkin' to the crick or the fish or the birds, the bugs and even the plants. In the fall of our first year I watched her from the barn sittin' up by the edge of the woods with a dozen deer feeding around her. During our thirty years together, I can't count the times she done that.

"I told Milly the only thing I worried about her goin' off alone was bears. The big black males can get real ornery ifn yer in their territory; and if females have youngens, they can be down right dangerous. She told me not to worry myself on account of she knew the bears hereabouts and they knew her. Edwards, from three farms up, stopped by one day perty excited. Said he was huntin' spring turkey early in the morning up on the ridge when he seen Milly walkin' along hummin' with a black bear amblin' behint her about twenty feet. Said he was gonna warn her when he realized they were together. 'Darndest thing!' he said. After that I didn't worry none.

"Another time she and me was walking downstream by the sycamores. She stopped and put her ear up agin the trunk of the tallest tree, and listened for a long time. She explained about trying to know what it was like to be that tree and have that smooth greeny-white skin and think the thoughts of the tree. Milly figured trees didn't think like us, but just felt things and maybe remembered those feelings for years and years. Sometimes she'd imagine she had roots and felt them growing deep into the earth like long toes. Said she could almost taste the dirt through 'em.

"That was her way. Milly wanted to know flowers and rocks and bugs the same as she knowd the trees. She wanted to know the water in the crick and the broken light from the sky that danced on the water, the secrets of the brown trout and the turtle and the kingfisher and the red-tail. And most of all she wanted to sense the 'connectedness' she called it of all things and be a part of that circle. Others thought she was touched, but I think she was least touched of any of us.

"Milly had a bad chill for weeks. The day before she passed, she got up out of bed, wrapped herself in an old quilt and went down to the crick. I'd been cuttin' firewood up on the mountain so it was late afternoon before I found her. She looked like an Indian girl sittin' on the bank. Her long black hair hung down to her waist. When I got close, I could hear her talkin' but couldn't make out what she was sayin'. I picked her up and headed for the house. It had started to snow, but she was warm and seemed very content. 'I was saying goodbye,' she said.

"I kept the woodstove hot all night. Milly was tryin' to comfort me when I shoulda been comfortin' her. She said she knew that she was dyin', and that it was as natural a thing as being born. 'I'll be in good company,' she told me.

"She was gone by sun up."

The old man was quiet for many minutes. I was, too. He reeled in his line, checked the worm and cast back in. The stream sang its silver notes over the stone rapids above the hole and moved quietly into deeper water.

He continued, "Then I found the letter she told me about, a sort of will with instructions to follow. By dark I had built a raised platform right across the crick there with a pile of cedar sticks and logs under it. I carried Milly down wrapped in that old quilt and laid her out. It was snowing pretty hard, but this kind of work makes no mind of weather. I read the poems she had marked, said my goodbyes and lit the brush. I set on the bank with the red and yellow firelight dancing like a celebration over the white ground. Mixed with the cracklin' of the fire was the talk of the crick rapids. Her smoke drifted off to the woods. I felt such a complicated feeling, a pang, a happy sadness.

"Come morning I swept the ashes into a milk pail and did as she asked. I walked the length of Skinner Crick from the lower bridge to the springhouse spreading her ashes as I went. She wouldn't have it no other way."

The old man and I fished in silence for a long while. I had so many questions to ask but kept quiet. Together we watched the stream. Its water moved blue-green along the cut bank and held in its delicate grasp the tall sycamores and an immense sky.

Annin Creek

Old Ma told me I should git myself over to Zack's place on Annin Creek and see if he kin do anything for me. So I hiked over the hill the next morning and found Zack splittin' wood. He was stripped to the waist, all shinny from sweat. His long gray ponytail was stuck to his back and his beard was matted with bits of wood chips lodged here and there.

I didn't spook him none cuz his dogs commenced to bark soon as I stepped into the clearing north of his cabin. He waved me in and swore at the dogs. The bunch of 'em went silent.

"Hey, John, you old farmer," he said. "Isn't this a beauty of a day! Will ya have a taste of coffee with me?"

By that he meant his mud-black special coffee with a little hair of the dog in it. "Sure, Zack," I said. "Old Ma sent me over to see ya on account of I ain't been fit to live with lately. She said you might be able to help me, but I doubt it."

Zack eyed me pretty careful, combed his beard with his fingers and poured out two cups of coffee from a soot black saucepan that had been boiling away on a fire he had going in the woodlot. He fetched a bottle of homemade whiskey from behind a woodpile. Each cup got two long shots. Zack struggled into his yellowed long underwear top, buried the ax in the choppin' block and asked, "What are the symptoms?"

19

"I don't know. Ma says I've been all quiet and moody. That I snap at the dog and talk out loud to myself. Guess you could say I been feelin' blue, sorry for myself cuz things ain't worked out the way they supposed to."

Zack never even hesitated a moment. "Well, the details won't hep none. Everyone's is different, but the symptoms is all the same. Let's say your woman ran off and you got yerself drunk and woke up with yer neighbor's wife, a woman you always held to be ugly and, waking up, you realized she was uglier than you thought. You felt like that ugliness had rubbed off on you. When you git home you find that yer best dog got hisself kilt in the road or, better yet, by a bear. You also discover that the cow went dry, an owl got into the chickens and the rent money is due with no hope in sight of payin' it.

"So now yer in a fix from several directions and hung over to boot. That'd be enough to cripple any growd man, even yerself. By the way, did you kill anyone?"

"No!" I said.

"Good. That always complicates things. So this should be easy. What you do is have a second cup of coffee and head for the creek. You take yer flyrod and go three bends down from here. Go in quiet cuz those trout are always listenin', they feels the vibration of steps right through the water. So if you go in softly and put on a Black Ghost or a Furnace Spider you have a chance. Its always better if you tied the flies yerself and, better still, if you used feathers from a poached pheasant, one ya got from a neighbor who's at the livestock auction in town or some darn place. Don't take it from the same guy with the ugly wife. He's got his own troubles and'll probly be comin' around here soon enough. If you was critical, I'd say build up your own rod, too, but you seem more salvageable than most.

"So ya got yer fly on. Ya got the sound of the rapids upstream from where you waded in. Ya got deep woods full of beech, birch and a few chestnut on the far bank, and behint ya is the field gone wild with gold 'n purple flowers, vines, weeds of every sort, thickets and scrub trees. You can smell the clover and realize why the bees is always so excited 'n focused on their sweet chores. Yer hearin' the lark, the jay, the kingfisher and, far in the woods, the drummin' of the grouse lookin' for a lady. The beech leaves is slightly tremblin' in a breeze you can't feel. You'll see a silver fox watchin' from the woods or maybe a coyote sniffin' the air.

"The stream will be full of sky, full of dancin' light. It'll dazzle ya like the fancy lure earrings the ladies in town wear. Work that line in the air to and fro, front and back. Easy now, feel the rhythm cuz that is what you've lost, and this cure wont take if you let yer brain spin around in a whirlpool of troubles. All you know in this here world is that line cuttin' the air in graceful arcs, to and fro, back and forth, swish, swish. Let it out a bit more and then a touch more. Be alert! Let that fly land like a piece of dust where the rapids ends and the pool begins. The water gets real still right there cuz it ain't sure of where to go. The fly will drift in the uncertain water, then twitch it just a little. Let it float some more, then another twitch.

"Probly the water will explode, and you'll have yerself a real battle. And if you are deserving, you'll land 'im. You see, in this situation you are the hunter. To be successful you have to have everything in balance. And that is the cure. Besides a fly caught trout tastes so much better than a dynamited trout. I've always found them that blasts fish out of the water are usually too far along the road to disaster to be helped. They'll drowned or get theirselves shot or end up in jail. Besides they never hear good afterwards. Sorry, I didn't mean to get so distracted on that subject."

"So what yer tellin' me," I said, "is to go fishin'?"

"Don't miss the point here, boy." Zack said. "Fishin' ain't the point. You've lost yer balance, fell off a log. Fishin' is the way you get that balance back. It takes you back to what is essential in life. Once you feels the rhythm of that rod and line, and sense the light on the water soaking into yer clothes, yer skin, then you can get yer priorities straight, realize again what's really important in this world. I could just come right out and tell ya what's worth it, but you ain't ready to receive it. Yer all turned around inside. Once you get yer innards straight, you won't need anyone to tell you anything! You'll get it yer own self, and before ya know it Old Ma will have here son back. Here, have one more coffee afore yer off."

I said, "Thanks, Zack. How long will this take?"

"Could be a day, a week or more dependin' on how bad off you are. Goes faster if you tie yer own flies and build yer own rod. Use that rod yer Pa built. And don't take no more whiskey with ya than needed to sweeten coffee. And don't bring no fish back either. Cook 'em up as soon as you pull 'em out, and eat them trout right there on the bank. It's the only cure I know, and for them that's followed it, it never failed."

Walking back up Finn Hollow and over the hill to home I thought of how to snare a pheasant, where I left my number ten hooks, my wicker creel and the broken fly rod my father built many years ago when he took the cure.

Lillibridge Creek

She came to me in a dream. I was napping just up valley a ways by Guy Hollow. Had been hiking the ridges all day and it was near nightfall. The creek pools near the hollow, and at the head of this little falls is a large flat rock. Good place to nap. It's cool in there even on a hot day like this one was.

My back was giving me some grief so I stretched it out on the rock. The whole trick for knowing the woods is to be still. I got real quiet. There was hardly any sky visible through the treetops. A red-tail was circling up there crying his lonesomeness. Turkeys were clucking on the ridge. A hermit thrush had begun its evening song, a sweet lullaby.

Bugs of every sort added to the chorus as well as all the other creatures that live in the stream. The air was fragrant with fern, moss and mountain laurel. I don't think I could have been more content. My eyes closed and I was left with listening and sniffing the air. There must have been deer bedded down nearby because I could smell their musk strong as spring skunk cabbage. After a while all the woods noise blended into one distant sound, a kind of earth song that had no words, just feelings to it. Soon enough I was asleep.

The dream itself was peculiar, seemed so real the way a dream will when you're deep into it. The 'she' I mentioned was a young girl of the Susquehannock people which is how she introduced herself. In the dream she came to the rock where I was sleeping and called out to me. She called me by name. I stood up, but my body stayed asleep on the rock. Looking back, I felt anxious leaving my body behind, but she kept calling, motioning me to come with her as if she had something for me to see.

I could see her clearly. Her dark hair hung in a long braid down her back tied with a woven leather strip, which also held a blue-gray falcon feather. A woven hide rope held her skin dress close at the waist. I remember she was barefoot. Her eyes were dark and steady set in a kind, oval face. The girl was tall and very beautiful.

The deer path we followed angled up the hillside through dense woods. I could feel the ferns brushing against my legs and the pressure of the stiff laurel branches as I pushed them aside in order to follow my guide. The deer asleep under a stand of pines did not stir at our passing. As if she knew my thoughts, the girl said, "They are dreaming of mild winters and full bellies. Their dreams are not so different from ours."

She touched trees as we passed them the way you'd touch the shoulder of a friend. I followed. The scent in the air changed as we gained altitude. At first wet with the odor of fern and pine, then leaf decay and laurel blossom, and now the aroma of wild grapes and raspberries as we approached a meadow. I've hiked these hills my whole life, but I did not recognize this place.

Saxifrage grew out of exposed rock, the small white flowers a testimony to their delicate strength. Foxgloves clustered about the base of the trees that bordered the field, as did the yellow ladyslippers. The opening in the woods was a two-acre painter's canvas filled with light. It was as if all of my senses were heightened. Bees drifted among large colonies of gold Hawkweed and yellow Day Lilies. I could hear their wing beats. Lobelia and Purple Loosestrife were spilled across the field like paint. Here and there were clouds of white blossoms from that wild carrot Queen Anne's Lace. Blueberry and raspberry bushes were lush and full of fruit. Swallows whistled as they darted through the air twisting into a sudden rise and then diving through the sky.

The Susquehannock girl said, "This is the place where Black Bear brings her cubs to feed on berries. They will be here this evening."

She breathed deep the flowery air and waded through the wild colors to the far woods. I followed. We cut through a ravine and ascended a steep slope. The trees were much taller now, and their thick canopy formed a solid ceiling blocking out the sky. The contrast from the brightness of the field was profound. I began to feel uneasy in this mid-day darkness, a sense that there were things in the deep shadows I did not understand, was not familiar with. There were spirits here, ancient ghosts hiding among the black boulders watching our movements.

The girl knew my anxiety and touched my shoulder the way she had been touching the trees. My fears evaporated, calm was restored. As we climbed, she pointed to fresh tracks of elk and wolf, animals that had not been seen in these parts for a hundred years. Beside a spring were cat tracks wider than my hand. In my imagination I could see this tawny colored cat crouched, drinking from the pool, its eyes squinting, ears alert. I had seen these tracks before when as a kid I tagged along with my dad on one of his bear hunts. Since that time the tracks had vanished.

The land began to level out. The girl led me along a ridge which headed toward town. The mountain I knew had hardwoods, but here we were walking among tall firs with trunks two people couldn't reach around. At the head of the mountain we came onto a bluff that gave a panoramic view of the valley. I felt totally disoriented. The village was gone. The railroad, the highway, the glass factories, the houses, the people; all gone. No sign of them. What I saw was a vast forest of white pine and hemlock covering the mountaintops and sides like a thick green rug. Most of these trees were better than a hundred fifty feet tall. The carpet changed in hue along the valley floor where maple, chestnut, oak and hickory trees grew in abundance, their leaves a silver-green in the crisp air. In a broad field along the riverbank, a dozen elk grazed like cattle. Winding its way along the valley floor, the Allegheny flowed full twice the width I knew it to be. From my vantage point, I could see where Portage Creek and Skinner Creek flowed into the river each the color of sky. Below to my left was silvery Lillibridge Creek, a gray snake pouring down the valley.

The air was alive with birds. The feathers of a rough-legged hawk fluttered as it rode the thermals coming off the mountain top. In the distance, the V shaped wings of turkey vultures circled lazily in the blue sky like large, black butterflies. Scarlet tanagers, rose-breasted grosbeaks and northern orioles whistled among the branches of nearby trees looking in their red and orange like ripe fruit. In the pine duff of the forest floor, rufous-sided towhees did their scratch dance looking for seeds and bugs all the while talking to each other in their melodic two-note tongue.

One of the things I remember most clearly wasn't anything I saw. It was the conflicting feelings inside. There was joy and sorrow side by side. The joy came from the view of the primitive Allegheny valley hundreds of years before we came. The sorrow was the loss of that rich land. I was keenly aware that I was in a dream and knew that if I stirred, everything would be lost. The river would cease to flow, the forest would recede into memory, the birds would leave the sky.

On the ground next to me was a flat smooth stone. Impressed in it was the fossil of a large seashell as fresh and perfect as a cat's track in mud. It's fan shape and radiating grooves appeared to have been carved by an artist. I pointed it out to the young Susquehannock girl who had been waiting nearby.

She moved close to me and let her fingers trace the delicate lines of the shell. She said, "In the early time the sea came here. This was before there were valleys. Then the sea went away. It left a great plain covered in grass with springs bubbling up from down below. The animals showed the springs where to flow, where the easy earth was. The water did its work and made the valleys. Then the trees came followed by the elk, the wolf and the bear. Where we are standing on this mountaintop was once the bottom of the sea."

Then she said, "It is time to go."

She took my hand and led me back along the dark ridge to the deer path that zigzagged down the hillside toward the meadow. It was evening, and the she bear had brought her cubs to feed on berries. They sat on their haunches stripping large pawfuls of raspberries from the bushes. So engrossed were they that they didn't even notice our passing. We went on through a more familiar part of the woods.

Soon I could hear the splash and laughter of Lillibridge Creek. The Susquehannock girl stopped and said, "I must leave you now. You'll be able to find your way back."

She turned and disappeared into the trees. I followed the dim path through ferns and laurel until I came to the waterfall and the large flat rock. There I was, still asleep on the rock. I laid down. For a long time I listened to the night sounds. A Great Horned Owl called from up Guy Hollow. Frogs bellowed from the edge of the pool. In the distance, a wolf howled from the ridge top. Deer moved slowly through the woods following the creek down the valley.

Twomile Creek

When we were young, the kids were always teasing Noah, a lanky farm boy. 'How's the boat comin', Noah?' 'I think it's going to rain, Noah.' 'I hear you gotta zoo up at that farm of yours, Noah.' I may have even done it myself, but he had long since forgiven me. He forgave everyone. When teased, he'd just smile accepting the joke, thereby, disarming the taunting child who always hoped for more of a reaction. Noah was too good-natured.

The teasing, though, was never far off. Noah wasn't building a boat, but he loved wild animals and birds and was forever bringing them home. His farm was just up the creek from the Mennonite church. His Ma had died when Noah was eight, but she had left him with the gift of the woods. She had had a way with animals and had passed that on to Noah.

His father, on the other hand, cursed Noah's collection of strays and cripples. On purpose, when Noah wasn't around, Papa would leave the gate open to the pen that held the fawn or leave the owl cage unlocked. But the fawn wouldn't leave and the owl remained on his perch, both preferring the safety of Noah's protection to the perils of the deep woods.

Noah told me about all this. He said Papa wasn't angry at the animals. He was angry at Ma for leaving him, angry that the farm wasn't making money, angry that he had to work in the glass plant which was full of noise, unnatural dirt and was inside. He hated being indoors. So he took all his bad feelings and hurled them at the snakes, the rabbits, the skunk and the red fox. Noah once caught his father kicking a cub bear out of his way. He had become a bitter man and, according to Noah, was injured just as real as if he were the Cooper's hawk in the barn with one wing blown off.

Noah knew too that sometimes with enough healing, an animal or bird could recover and even, in some cases, be returned to the wild. And in other cases, they died. The latter was true for his father.

Noah told me at graduation that Papa couldn't come because he had to work the 'goddamn day shift'. Noah wasn't embarrassed, the way a town kid would have been, that he had to drive himself to the ceremonies in the old Chevy truck that had no doors, no paint and smelled of manure. He had to be proud all by himself when the principal announced, "The Port Allegany Science Prize goes to Noah Smith of Twomile Creek for his excellent work in biology!" Of course, I told him that I was proud of him. He shook my hand, smiled and drove off.

He had invited me to come out to the farm for some dinner and a taste of Papa's home brew after my family's picnic was over. When I got there, I found him in his father's room holding Papa's hand. Papa was dead. I had never seen Noah cry before.

"What happened?" I said.

"I knew something was wrong when I got home and saw Papa's car by the barn. It was parked funny and the door was open. He wasn't even supposed to be home from work yet. I found him on the floor by the woodstove all curled up. He looked so small the way a bird looks when all the life has gone out of it.

"He wanted a drink of whiskey which I gave him. He said he was getting hard pains in his chest while he was at work. They sent him home. He was conscious long enough to tell me how sorry he was for everything, sorry for missing graduation, sorry for mistreating the critters, and sorry for not doing better by me. I told him about the science prize and showed him the twenty-five dollar check and the certificate. He hugged me for that. Then he went to sleep, and just drifted away."

We sat together for several hours until the undertaker came. There was red dust on the white hearse from the clay road that led to the farm. After it drove away, Noah and I fed all the 'critters'.

So that was many years ago. I had gone away to school and, afterwards, moved up into the Finger Lakes of New York. But I visited home often and always took a drive up Twomile Creek to see if Noah was around.

On every visit there was something new. Noah had become an unofficial veterinarian. Not only did he care for injured and abandoned wild things, but other farmers and towns people, the same ones who used to tease him when we were kids, began bringing him their sick animals. He was called to farms to help with difficult births when a calf got turned around inside its mother. Dogs hit by cars or with porcupine needles protruding from their noses and cats with tapeworms showed up at his door.

I was there one afternoon the summer we were both thirty when a young girl showed up having walked all the way from town carrying her kitten who had gotten caught in a lawn mower and had a mangled leg. The young girl was covered with blood. She couldn't speak; she just held the half dead kitten out to Noah. He took it into the barn part of which had been converted into an operating room and went to work. I stayed outside with the girl trying to distract her by showing her the new bear cub just a few months old, the three-legged fox that had chewed off its own leg to escape a steel trap and the blind turkey buzzard named Elizabeth.

"That's my name," the girl said. "But they call me Lizzy."

We also went to the deer pen. In it were two fawns and a yearling. The yearling was limping badly. It had a wooden splint on its front left leg. Noah came out just then. "What happened to the deer?" Lizzy asked.

"He made the mistake of playing in the road. I saw him get hit over near Turtle Point," Noah explained. "For a while, it didn't look like he was going to make it. The bone was pretty badly shattered. But he should be ready to have that splint off today. Would you like to help?"

"Yes," she said.

Noah told Lizzy to pet the deer's nose and keep looking into his eyes while he cut the tape that held the splint. She did so, and the deer never flinched. While Noah was massaging the deer's leg, Lizzy asked about her kitten as if she didn't really want to know the answer.

Noah said that he couldn't save the leg, but the rest of the cat would be fine. The girl gave him a big hug. "She'll have to stay here a week or so to recuperate. Now, I've known many three legged cats that get along just fine. In fact, I have one up at the house. His name is Tripod."

Noah had certainly found his place. He was able to make a comfortable living doing just what he had always done. He had an extensive library in the house filled with the writings of Muir, Burroughs, Audubon, and Leopold as well as medical books on the care of animals. Two of the books he had written himself. *How to Repair a Broken Wing* detailed his methods for caring for injured birds. *The Fox with No Tail* did the same for wild animals. Out by the main road, Noah had attached a barn board to the mailbox post. Printed in barn red letters was the name he had given the farm: *The Ark.*

———

Last summer, Noah celebrated turning forty-five by getting married to a thirty-year old girl who 'loves all things wild!' he told me. It was a perfect match. Her name is Elizabeth. Noah told me that Liz went with him on all his calls and was an excellent assistant. He said I had met her once before when she brought an injured cat to him. I remembered.

This past winter I visited my folks on Pearl Street for the Christmas holidays. Noah and Liz had invited me for New Year's Eve dinner. Liz called at seven and said they had to cancel because they had gotten a call to come out to a big barn fire out on Combs Creek. The farmer had lost thirty head of cattle. A few cows and a couple of horses had gotten out but were in bad shape. The farmer wanted Noah to see if there was anything he could do or to destroy the ones that couldn't be saved. I understood.

A little after one in the morning, Liz called again. She was in tears. I could barely understand her. What I did hear was that something tragic had happened at the Ark, that Noah needed me and that I should bring my old rifle.

The night was bitter cold and, except for where the hills were, the stars shown like ice. The road along the creek was slippery. My headlights were reflected in the silver eyes of deer feeding on shrubs growing by the water. The creek itself was too fast at the head of the valley to freeze over. I wondered how Noah's two snow geese were doing on a night like this. The female had a broken wing, which Noah had set. The male had stayed on living up to its loyal reputation.

Liz was waiting for me at the head of their road by the mailbox. She got in still crying.

"Liz, what is it? Where's Noah? Is he all right?" I asked.

She stammered, "He's not here. Drive up to the barn and you'll see."

The headlights swept the snowy field. The house and barn lights cast silver shafts out onto the yard. Dark lumps lay strewn across the frozen ground. I was afraid of what it was I was about to see. Lying in front of the car were the two geese, their carcasses shredded, feathers and blood stuck to the snow. Further on was a fawn crumpled in two pieces. The silver fox was still in its pen, lifeless, limp as cloth. A Great Horned Owl and a Cooper's hawk were torn apart by the barn door. Three other deer were dead in their pen, and, in a nearby cage, a blue tick hound that had been recuperating from having its ear sewn back on after an encounter with a bear lay dead. The scent of entrails permeated the frozen air. Dead chickens and ducks were everywhere. Cages were caved in and broken glass stuck out of the snow like thin ice. On the front porch looking as if he had been trying to get into the house was a cub bear, his crimson blood spattered on the wall.

I looked at Liz. "Where's Noah?"

"He went after them," she whispered.

"Them who?" I said.

"The dogs. He said it was a pack of wild dogs. He could tell from the tracks. Three of them were big, the other five were smaller."

"Is he on foot?"

"No, he took one of the horses. He asked me to call you to see if you'd try to catch up with him. The dogs couldn't get in the barn, so both horses are okay. I saddled up the mare if you want to try to find Noah."

I could hear a whimpering coming from under the porch. I scooted under with the flashlight and pulled out a year old bobcat. Its eyes were wide and it wouldn't uncurl itself. Liz gently took it from me and began to weep again. The cat is the only thing that had survived the attack. Liz looked the way she had so many years ago when she brought the injured kitten to Noah.

Liz wiped at her eyes and said, "We found this when we got home from the fire. I hadn't seen Noah cry before. It was as if he'd been torn apart by those dogs. He said he could hear the cries of the animals and feel their terror, feel their skin tear and bones snap. He went in the house and got a rifle I don't think he's ever used. I could tell there'd be no stopping him. He said by dawn the tracks would be swept away. There were several shots up near the head of the valley just before you got here. Will you try to find him for me?"

"Of course," I said.

I didn't want to leave her there amidst that carnage, so I backed the old Chevy truck out of the barn and cleared things away. Liz gave me a flashlight and said, "Noah said the tracks led upstream. He figured they were headed for Lillibridge or Sartwell Creek."

It was easy to follow his tracks up the valley. It was cold though, well below zero. The mare slipped occasionally on ice under the snow. Her breath and mine puffed out in great clouds as we angled our way up the hillside toward the crest overlooking Lillibridge. The stiff mountain laurel scratched at my legs like bony fingers trying to grab me and pull me off the horse. Low pine boughs and bare limbs of oak and maple slashed at my face. The only other sounds in the still woods were muffled hooves in the snow, the creaking of the leather saddle and me talking softly to the horse trying to reassure her and me that those dogs had not circled back and were not about to pounce on us.

The borrowed light of the snow helped us to find our way. We crossed a spring near the crest and passed through a thick stand of spruce trees. Just as we reentered the hardwoods, the horse whinnied and I spotted the first of the dogs. Three of them, one shepherd and two mongrels, were lying where they fell, their chests covered in blood. Each muzzle was smeared with a crimson stain, evidence of their earlier deed. Noah must have been crazed with anger. Liz was wrong about one thing; he certainly knew how to use that rifle.

I hadn't shot my 30-40 Craig since I was fourteen. We were hunting deer up Strang Hollow. Five of us, four uncles and me, were slow walking through the woods late in the day. A buck was following behind us. I was the first to see it. I turned and fired. The deer went down, I went down. The deer got up; I got up. I fired. The deer went down, I went down. The deer got up and bounded off. One of my uncles found a blood trail. We waited a half hour for the deer to lie down. Using candles, we followed that trail 'til two in the morning and never found the deer. My uncle explained that once the deer did lie down, he wouldn't get up again. Death would come soon. What a terrible waste I had told him. He said that nothing is wasted in the woods. Just the same, I never hunted after that until this night.

The mare and I slid down into Lillibridge. Six shots came from a half mile away near where the creek breaks out of the woods into a pasture. The echo of each shot ricocheted around the valley and up Hardes Hollow. By the time I got to the creek, Noah was gone but four dogs lay sprawled in their final death leap. These had not been healthy animals. One was a battle-scarred boxer. The other three were mutts with mangy fur all matted with burrs. Open sores on each oozed a clear liquid. Blood was spilled on the snow.

I caught up with Noah on the town road that paralleled Lillibridge Creek. He said he was glad to see me. Rather than say anything about what had happened back at the farm, I said, "Where'd you learn to shoot like that?"

"Papa always said that knowing how to shoot doesn't mean you have to, but if you have to, you better know how. You must think I'm touched being out here in the middle of the night."

"A little maybe, but you've got just cause. By my count, there's only one left."

"You count good. I saw this last one. May even have hit him. He's a big black shepherd mixed with something else. Missing an eye I think. Did you notice anything strange about all that killin' back at the farm?"

I said, "I noticed it was complete except I found the bobcat under the porch. He was okay."

"Oh, that's good news. Liz loved that thing as if it were her own child. She was sure they had dragged it off. The reason I knew it was dogs was that nothing was eaten. It was killing for killing's sake. There is a lot that's violent in nature, but it is always for a reason. The whole thing is set up for one thing to feed on another, the strong attack the weak, the quick devour the slow. But these dogs weren't hungry. It was plain bloodlust.

"Any animal raised from birth in the wild knows to kill for food or in self defense. But these town dogs gone wild don't know that. And it's not even the dog's fault. Owners who can't find them homes or can't put them down abandon them up there at the Lookout. It's the owners we ought to be hunting tonight. They're the sons-a-bitches who should be lying out there in the field by the creek. These mangy dogs are victims same as my animals. They lived under a contract that said the humans promised to care for them and, in turn, the dogs would forget their wild ancestry. The humans broke their promise when they dumped these poor curs back in the hills.

"These dogs were just getting revenge the same as I'm doing tonight. I've seen their kills in the woods before. Just a few weeks back over on Long Branch near Annin Creek I found a deer torn to shreds. Nothing was eaten. Now a deer expects to be taken by a coyote and will forgive him because he knows it's the way things are. But the deer no more understands wild dogs than that old pair of geese did back home.

"The black dog went up the hollow road. I've been pushing him pretty hard, so he should be about wore out. He knows I know him, and I know he knows me. Let's go."

I trotted behind Noah whose flashlight traced the long strides of the black dog. The road had not been plowed for several weeks so the deep tracks were easy to follow. Noah looked like a figure cut from an early American novel: a trapper-hunter, fur cap, long canvas coat, leather gloves, reins in one hand, rifle in the other. The road stopped a mile and a half up the hollow at a camp that was only used during hunting season.

The tracks did not stop. The black one was heading for the upper hollow which I knew to be narrow and a hard hike on foot in daylight. Noah said we'd take the horses in as far as we could then go on on foot.

We had gone in about a quarter of a mile on a deer trail when the land on either side got very steep. I couldn't see past Noah, but I heard him shout, "There he is!" Two shots rang out like cannon fire shattering the silent dark. "HeeYah!" yelled Noah urging his timid horse into a run. A hundred yards up he waited for me. Noah pointed his light at the blood in the snow.

"He'll be easy enough to follow now. We'll wait a bit to see if he holes up. Once down, he won't get up again," said Noah. That idea sounded familiar.

The horses shuffled their feet nervously as we waited in the dim, gray light of the gully. The stars were shards of ice hanging from the trees above. An eerie silence fell upon us like a thick blanket. Nothing stirred the frigid night air. Then Noah whispered, "Did you hear that?" He clicked off the safety of his rifle. I did the same.

At first I hadn't heard it. The low growl was so faint that it seemed to be coming from deep in my own startled imagination. It was a primitive, guttural sound, one, ancient men must have shuddered to hear. The hair on the back of my neck stood up and my heart went weak. The horses whined. Noah spoke to them and me, "Easy now, easy there. He has become the hunter again. He's coming for us. Be ready."

The growl grew in intensity. Its blood notes filled the night like thunder. A desperate voice speaking of many kills.

The black dog was a shadow among shadows as it leapt from the ledge above us, its final notes mortar fire meant to paralyze its victim. Before either of us could fire a shot, he hit Noah full force knocking him off his horse. The two tumbled to the ground. Noah's rifle stuck barrel first in the snow. The mustang bucked wildly kicking the dog away from Noah towards me. It scrambled to its feet snarling. I fired. The recoil nearly knocked me off my horse. The dog yelped and fell limp in the snow.

Noah was kneeling next to the dog. Blood was dripping from a gash in his left cheek. He spoke quietly to the dog, "I forgive you, dog. I forgive you."

The mustang had run off so Noah got up on the mare behind me. Slowly we worked our way down to the hollow road. We did not speak. Creaking leather and the shuffling hooves of the horse were the only sounds. The icy stars over the valley kept their vigil until they were swallowed by the hills.

Combs Creek

Jed McAllister sat on a gray log by a section of Combs Creek where the rapids led into a deep pool. He was studying the early morning light on the water and its reflection on silver maple leaves. In the fast water of the rapids some of the light was swallowed by dark gray-green hesitations that looked like pools of mercury behind the large rocks. Other light ricocheted into a silver spray riding columns of blue like lyrics floating above notes in a song.

Jed watched the moss green of the deeper pool, which wrinkled in concentric circles where brook trout split the surface feeding on stranded mayflies that had hatched during the night. A slight breeze caused the silver maple leaves to twitch and the tall grass to bow.

Mixed with the light, Jed noticed the hum of insects, the groan of frogs, the chattering of gray squirrels and the talk of many birds. The flickers shrill cry, the catbirds whine, the hoarse voice of the grackle and the coo of the mourning doves were notes in sync with the dance and caesura of the light. Jed was memorizing the currents, the way the water moved, the flow of sound upstream and down. After a time he even felt as though he could sense the subtle air currents as they pressed the maple leaves, and drew wedges on the surface of the pool as if a fin from below were passing. These same invisible streams of air carried the perfume of the field with its bouquet of wildflowers: wild ginger, mint and clover as well as purple loosestrife, goldenrod and strawberries. The creek gave off its scent of things mossy and decaying, of things wriggling to life and staring out of their watery world at Jed as he sat staring back.

An hour passed. Two hours. Jed knew he had slipped into one of his meditations, an attempt to lose the self in order to gain the self. More and more he had come to know that his long periods of stillness had a purpose and that it was not laziness or a refusal to acknowledge responsibility. It was just his way. Whether sitting for half a day on the front porch of the farmhouse to watch rain fall in the valley or spending hours in the evening near the old orchard by the barn to see the sunlight go off the mountain, Jed was absorbing what was before him. He took in detail the way most people breathed in air: subtle things like the way a rufous-sided towhee will scratch dance a sort of one-step to turn leaves to find seed or grubs, or the way strong light will pass through a sugar maple leaf so that the shadow will also show intricate veins, a road map spread out on a piece of lichen covered granite.

Jed reached for the oak case he had built to carry his journal, paints, tripod and canvas. The honey colored box was dovetailed on the corners, had a brass latch to secure the hinged lid and a handle made from a piece of bridle fastened with copper tacks. A spring-loaded clamp was attached to the outer top edge of the lid for holding a canvas in place. The bottom edge had a grooved, protruding lip where he could rest one brush while using another. On the back of the case, a large triangular piece of leather was held fast on the upper two sides by more copper tacks. This created an envelope that would easily slide over the top of the tripod giving Jed a firm surface on which to paint. In almost a child's scrawl, Jed had burned his name and Combs Creek on the lid with a soldering iron.

He unpacked the box placing a half dozen tubes of paint on the log to his right and next to those a piece of slate he had found over in Strang Hollow which he now used as a palette. Beside the slate he balanced a tin soup can, which contained eight brushes. On the log to his left, he placed the composition book, which was his journal. He unfolded the legs of the tripod and slid the five inch copper tubing over each hinge to keep the legs from buckling. Jed spread the legs so that the bailing wire was taut and slid the case down into position. He unrolled a piece of canvas and clamped it to the case. Each of these steps was part of a ritual, which helped him prepare for painting. He was ready to begin.

Jed used a carpenter's pencil to do the initial sketching. The stream spilled across the center with its rapids and pool. The maple tree appeared to the right hanging over the slow water. A thicket of sumac grew up on the far bank leaning upstream in the breeze. Further back from the creek, daises and asters appeared surrounding a wild rose bush. The canvas air stirred with the humming and buzzing of insects, swallows swooping and a kestrel fluttering above the field searching for grasshoppers.

There was never any certainty for Jed whether or not the way he went about painting was the right way to do it. He had never had any training of any sort so he just created from instinct. Through experimentation with hundreds of paintings, he had uncovered his own method and stuck to it. He had loved to draw ever since he was a child. Now he was trying to recall when the painting started. As he worked with the yellows, reds, blues, greens and shades of gray, he thought about his journal. Keeping it was a habit developed simultaneously with the painting. Now that he was in a state of clear thinking, all the murky details of the past twelve years temporarily swept aside or settled at the bottom out of sight, Jed was able to recall the source of his passion for capturing in acrylic and words his excursions into the wilds and into himself.

It had become his routine to write an entry after every painting. The entries cataloged plants, sky and weather conditions, encounters with wild animals especially black bears and the rare mountain cats, and observations on the connectedness of all things including his own relationship with the valley. He also recorded struggling thoughts, evolving answers to a myriad of life's tough questions.

The source, he realized, dated back to the spring of 1940, two years before he lost his parents in the flood, two years before he had to take over a half ruined farm rather than go on to normal school to study science and art, two years before he would be on his own fending for himself. It was the spring of his junior year at the Arnold Avenue School.

Often while hiking deep in the remote areas of the Allegheny Plateau where he was observing red bellied trout in the beaver ponds, following a large flock of wild turkeys or tracking a coyote, Jed would meet up with Myron Weimer, a banker from the village. The two wanderers would exchange stories, and Myron would share the mushrooms he had picked.

As Jed thought about Myron, he mixed a little white with blue and began to fill in the sky of his painting and places on the creek water where the sky floated.

One morning when the two met up Cady Hollow, which was just over the hill from Jed's farm, Myron invited him to stop by the bank to see a journal that his wife's great-great-grandfather had kept. After school the following day Jed held in his hands the leather bound nature diary of Jedediah Evans. The first entry, dated May 12, 1851, was written in graceful script:

> *The dogs cornered a bear up Leman Hollow near Sartwell Creek just after sun up. Hazel my favorite shepherd for seven years and a damn good hunter had her throat slashed and was dead on the spot. Albert, One Eye, Crazy and Ginger were so tore up I had to shoot em after I took the bear. All five dogs was the best cept for One Eye. For a coonhound he wasn't worth much. Just a follower. Now I'm down to 24 dogs.*
>
> *The he bear went a little over 500 pounds dressed. Good fur, should fetch 10 dollars. Stomach was full of berries dried and hard left over from last year and what looked like deer meat but it was hard to tell. Built a tote to drag him out to where the horse was hitched down by the creek which I did after I buried the dogs. The other five dogs ate the bear innards cept for the heart and livers which I kept for myself. The kill took place in a hardwood with many large ferns and a thick patch of groundpine. It was cool this morning and the sky was empty blue.*

What impressed Jed even more than the writing was the ink drawing at the bottom of the page of a black bear rearing up fighting off nine dogs. Hazel already lay dead in the leaves. Next to that drawing were smaller sketches of ferns, groundpine, some mushrooms and a raven or crow.

Jed daubed several shades of gray and white on the canvas to capture the light refracting off the rapids. He continued almost unconsciously as the details of Jedediah's log flowed back to him.

Myron said to Jed, "I thought you might like to see that. You and old Jedediah have the same first name and similar interests. What I find remarkable is that the old hunter could read and write and draw. Look ahead to that entry for August first of that first year."

Jed leafed through to that page and read:

> *The goddam loggers have clearcut the front slopes of all the hills that face the river. The animals can't live there no more. The greedy bastards didn't leave a stick standing. The mountain cats, bears, elks and wolfs will have to go deeper into the rough woods until the money hungry louts cut roads back there. The heavy rain all July has turned the River to mud. I'll bet the muskellunge can't even breathe in that roily water. When the hills dries out the slash will burn for months. What a sadness has laid upon me.*

The drawing below this brief entry was of a wasteland, hills covered with stumps like severed arms and a black Allegheny River oozing through the center, a sinister black snake making its way through the spoiled valley. On one ridge, a gray wolf stood as a witness.

Myron had said that 'the wife' wouldn't allow the journal to be loaned out, but that Jed was more than welcome to stop by any time and read it. Jed recalled doing just that every day for weeks until he read all the entries, which spanned a ten-year period from 1851 to 1861. Jedediah Evans had recorded the births and deaths of his dogs, their ancestry and the hunting skill or lack thereof for each. Each hunt included the names of the dogs that accompanied him; whether a bear, cat, elk, white-tail or wolf was bagged; and his 'reading' of the contents of the stomach. He wrote about plants at the location of the kill and the weather conditions, storm or calm. Often he listed what he fed his dogs which mainly consisted of carp, snapping turtle, ground 'possum and bear meat.

Each entry was accompanied by what Jedediah called in his log 'likenesses'. The drawings, done with a quill pen, depicted each kill, his cabin which was situated on a flat wedge of land where Combs Creek flows into Portage Creek, his bark canoe, traps with a map showing the

location of each, dogs, trees, flowers, shrubs, raptors, fish caught
especially muskellunge, fishing tackle, a collection of repeating rifles
and skinning knives and many other objects of Jedediah's daily life.

Everything was drawn in minute detail, the fishing tackle was
especially so. This morning Jed remembered the muskie lures which
Jedediah had carved out of wood. One was a duckling with paddle feet
that moved as it was drawn across the surface of the river. Similarly, a
mouse lure had moving feet in front and back. Listed next to these
drawings were lengths and weights: *3 feet 10 inches, 22 pounds; 5 feet
2 inches, 37 pounds, both taken September 3, 1854 from Allegheny
River down from Lillibridge.*

Jed changed from a medium brush to a very fine horsehair brush in
order to paint the slender stalks and delicate heads of the bottlebrush
and Indian grasses along the bank of the creek.

The final thing that Jed remembered about the log were statements
in quotes at the end of most entries or written in the margins. Jed wasn't
sure whether Jedediah Evans was quoting someone else or from a book
or if these were Jedediah's own thoughts to himself:

> *One is most alive just before death
> said the angry bear.*
>
> *A redbellied trout taken from a beaver
> pond tastes best if cooked and eaten
> before you bait your hook again.*
>
> *Human beings are as much a part of
> nature as oak trees and mountain cats
> although they often forget it.*
>
> *Kill the land and you are killing
> yourself.*
>
> *Carp make good fertilizer for squash
> and excellent food for dogs in winter.*

Jed McAllister stood up and stepped back from his painting. He
was pleased. Pleased with his thinking of the past several hours,
pleased with what he had captured on canvas. Having cleaned the
brushes and scraped the excess paint from the slate into a lidded
canning jar, Jed picked up his own journal and wrote the following
entry in as neat a hand as he could muster:

July 28, 1952

Today I escaped chores at the farm and spent the morning painting a picture of the section of Combs Creek that skirts the west field. While painting the rapids and pool, I renewed my acquaintance with Jedediah Evans whom I had first met in 1940 in the town bank office of Myron Weimer. Jedediah had died at Gettysburg, but before that kept an account of his fishing and hunting experiences during the 1850's. Myron showed me that log in his office.

The journal taught me many things, some which I knew but didn't think were of any use. Writing and drawing the details of a life gives you a deeper understanding of the intricacies of nature and the complex web of thought that lies within the mind and heart. Furthermore, each forces you into a calm place like the backwater of a fast stream where thought is inspired and imagination blooms like wildflowers in an untamed field.

Jedediah Evans showed me that when you write or draw, the words or ink or paint should capture more than just what is before you. They should carry the scent in the air, the sound of leaves vibrating, the play of light on water and the feeling that erupts as you witness the movements of nature's myriad cycles.
Today Jedediah was with me as I worked. It was good to have company. I think he liked Combs Creek Portrait.

Before he closed his journal, Jed sketched the painting on the page with that day's entry as he had done with all his entries over the past dozen years. In a far corner he added a 'likeness' of a gray wolf off in the distance looking down the valley where the creek tumbled and flowed its way into a thick stand of pines.

Bear Creek

Clara Hill sat on a stump near the cabin humming to herself while skinning a rabbit. She drew the knife along the belly from vent to chin, made a few slits up each leg and peeled the coat back as if removing a jacket. Later she would tack the pelt to the side of the cabin. She wiped sweat from her forehead with the rolled sleeve of her gray and white plaid shirt. Another slice up the belly and the innards spilled out into a blue enameled basin, which she placed within reach of the two whining dogs, Curly and Spike. Clara used the ax to sever the head and tossed it up in the woods for the raccoons.

Her hands were glazed with sticky blood. She washed them and the carcass in the spill water, which sloshed over the stone and sod dam that Edward had built ten years ago. He had stocked the pool above the dam with brook trout caught down in Sartwell Creek and over the hill in Fishing Creek.

It's too hot to cook indoors, she thought. Clara built up the fire, which had been smoldering in the fire pit since early morning. She skewered the rabbit on the spit above the flames. The pit was close enough to the stump that she was able to sit and turn the rabbit. Its little body, all white chords and muscle the color of a bruise, steamed as it rotated. She reached behind her back and tugged on the end of her long braid, an automatic habit.

Clara thought about Edward gone these five years. The accident had happened on her thirtieth birthday, their sixth year together. The stump she was resting on was once a hundred foot elm, which leaned precariously over their plank sided cabin threatening to crush it if it fell. The tree was mostly dead when Edward said it had to come down.

He climbed half way up the tree and attached two lines which he tied in turn to other trees explaining that when the elm fell the lines would guide it away from the cabin. It was a good idea, but Clara said he should wait 'til his brother came up on Saturday. He had a team of workhorses that could just pull the tree down. "This ain't that big a deal, Clara." was the last thing he had said.

Clara thought now how odd it was with memory how certain details stood out so over other ones. She remembered watching from up by the dam where the trout were jumping after dark flies causing the sky floating on the pool to undulate. She could still hear distinctly the kachunk, kachunk of the double bladed ax as Edward wedged the tree on the side facing the guide lines. He waved to her just before the sawing began. Halfway through the tree, the saw got stuck. Edward headed for the shed to get his steel wedges. The tree groaned. Edward turned and looked. The tree lurched, cracking with a sudden clap of thunder. This was followed by two smaller snaps like echoes, the guide lines breaking like old fish line.

The tree crumpled like a shot bear toward Edward. He had his hands up as if he could catch it, Clara remembered. The ground shook and dust curled in brown clouds about the dooryard. Clara jerked as she remembered how the ground moved. How afterward an intense silence had moved in. She could not even hear the waterfalls sloshing beside her. She could only see one of Edward's legs sticking out like a limb from under the immense trunk. Clara recalled how she sat down where she was and stayed there for several hours. Nothing else could be done.

Above her now crows cawed in the treetops. A hummingbird flew by, the whir of its wings, a released bowstring. Blue jays complained from the old apple orchard. A rough-legged hawk scratched the blue skin of the sky with its sharp descending whistle.

The sun had already begun to slip down the far side of the world leaving Clara in shadow. The steep hillsides were tarnished gold in the late day light. The fire crackled and spit yellow flames under the dripping rabbit. Smoke billowed up among the treetops in gray blue spirals. Clara was still thinking about Edward when she heard the churn of a truck engine coming up the gravel road.

She figured it must be Edward's brother checking up on her as he did every two weeks or so. Each time he visited, he'd bring her some supplies and try to talk her into moving to town. "It's no good for a handsome woman like yerself to waste away in this wild place all alone. Something could happen, 'n you'd be weeks gettin' help. Why, what if some wandering stranger happened by and decided to do you wrong? What then, Little Sis?"

"Saul, I got three rifles, a twelve gauge and a pair of pistols in the cabin there. I can drill a hopping rabbit through the ears at fifty paces. I don't think anyone's going to mess with me!"

Clara thought that she would tell Saul when he got there that if this rabbit could talk, he'd testify to her marksmanship. One of the things that gave her real pride in her life these days was her ability to take care of herself. Five years alone up this narrow valley had given her plenty of opportunity to test her resolve to stay on at the homestead. Winter storms, spring floods, summer drought, bears in the kitchen, mountain cats in the coop, firewood to be cut, garden to tend, sickness to be cured, injuries to be doctored. She hadn't even been to town going on three years.

She would tell Saul all this when he got there. Today had been a rare indulgence to remember Edward's accident so clearly. But memory, she thought, didn't make you weak unless you lived there.

An old, forest green pickup came into view. One headlight out, grill askew, three rifles in the gun rack, insignia on the caved in door. Clara stood up. This was not Saul's truck. She recognized it though. Bill Pearson was the local game warden. He had two other men with him. All three were in moss green uniforms. In the bed of the truck were two bloodhounds wriggling excitedly. The men slid out of the truck, pistols strapped to their sides.

"Hey, Clara," Bill smiled. "Haven't seen you in quite a spell. This here is Lyle Harper and Joe Beckman."

"Hey guys, how's it going?" Clara said as she moved between them and the fire where the rabbit sizzled.

"How do, miss," the two said.

"Something sure does smell good," Bill continued. "Whatcha cookin' there?"

Clara said, "The last of my dogs. I only got two left now."

"Mighty puny dog, Clara. Looks more like a rabbit."

"Well, to tell the truth it is. An old one though. Hopped right on in here and keeled over. Died of natural causes. Heart attack, I suspect."

Bill smiled again, "If that don't beat all. Relax, Clara. We ain't up here to spy on you. Fact is, the boys and I have us a situation. We hoped you could help us out some."

"If there's anything I can do, it'll be done," Clara said.

Joe Beckman explained, "We got two missing kids. A sister and brother. April and Philip Larkin from down to Burtville. You know, they got the chicken farm by the river."

Clara said, "I know them well. Edward always got our eggs there before we got the layers. Haven't seen that bunch in a while. How old's them kids now?"

"The girl is sixteen and the boy is twelve," Lyle said. "They been gone since yesterdy morning."

Clara frowned, "How'd this all happen?"

Bill said, "According to their folks, the kids went off Saturday morning hunting squirrels with the new .22 rifle the boy got as a gift. Squirrels is not even in season for Christ's sake! The father said he was sure they went up Hobson Hollow, which is all hickory, oak and chestnut, as you know. There's a lot of country up that hollow and back along this hill. We had the whole Roulette fire depart up there searchin' on foot and horseback. Even had one guy searchin' from his airplane. Lyle here is the only one to find tracks. They was in a mud bank nearly three miles in. The dogs lost the trail near the beaver pond. No other sign of them. We have a diver on his way to the pond to see if their bodies are anchored at the bottom. I sure hope he don't find 'em there."

"So you really have no idea what happened," said Clara.

"That's right," said Joe. "But we think either some one got those kids, did stuff we don't dare think about, kilt and buried 'em somewhere or they had an accident of their own making. Either way it don't look good. You seen anyone around here in the past few weeks?"

"Haven't seen a soul for months 'cept Saul, Edward's brother, who looks in on me once in a while to see if I'm dead yet or if I'm willin' to move into town. You guys hungry?"

Bill said, "Yes'm, we could go for a bite. You got a beautiful place right here. No sense movin' anywhere. We'd be much obliged if you'd keep yer eyes and ears peeled for anything unusual. Be careful though, if some slime of a human being messed with those kids, he may still be around."

She assured them that she'd keep an eye out and even hike up the mountain and have a look see first thing in the morning. She quartered the rabbit and shared it with the three men. Bill said, "It tastes mighty tender for an old rabbit who died of natural causes."

——— ——— ———

Clara did not sleep well. The bed squeaked as she rolled one way, then the other. She opened her eyes in the dark to see planks of moonlight lying on the bedroom floor. Owls talked out in the silver woods. The waterfalls gurgled and chugged its liquid notes in the white light. All the while the imagined details of the children's ordeal swept through Clara's head, each scenario worse than the preceding one.

She saw April and Philip separated from each other, clothes ripped, skin slashed from briars, blood trickling down their faces, each calling for the other in weaker and weaker voices. She saw them cornered against rocks by that wounded he bear that had been half shot over in Fishing Creek last week. In her semi-dream Clara saw the boy trip on a tree root, lurch forward accidentally discharging his new rifle into the back of his sister.

Clara shook at the sound of the rifle shot and sat up in bed. All was still and quiet. This ain't going to work, she thought to herself. It would be hours before daylight. She figured it must be around one in the morning. Clara lit the lantern, pulled on her clothes and began to pack her canvas rucksack. Venison jerky, a jug of water, strips of cloth for bandages, tape and salve, matches, her bone handled skinning knife, a coil of rope, and two boxes of cartridges, one for the Winchester .30-06 and the other for the old long barreled .32 Colt pistol.

She checked the flashlight. Batteries dead and corroded. What was that poem Edward was forever reciting, "Look for me by moonlight, I'll come to thee by moonlight, though hell should bar the way!" Edward would like the adventure of all this. So I'll travel by moonlight, Clara thought to herself as she strapped on the Colt and took the Winchester off the antler rack.

Outside the air was cool, the woods the color of milk. Clara stood still for several minutes to allow her eyes to adjust to the dim light. Curly and Spike stirred questioningly. Clara dropped bones near them so that they would not bark at her leaving. The trail led up by the waterfalls, which sparkled like fireflies, past the pool where the moon floated like a single eye, and followed Bear Creek into the hardwoods. Edward had told her that for hundreds of years animals used this path to get from hilltop to valley during the night. She could still hear his voice clearly and imagined a parade of bears and mountain cats just ahead of her. "I have a real bad feeling about this, Edward," she said aloud. Clara's hand fumbled in the dark as she checked the safety on the Winchester slung over her shoulder.

The trail was a gradual incline for the first mile. Very little of the moon's light penetrated the thick leaf cover above. The stream had diminished to a freshet, its narrow banks squeezing the water through tight, twisting rock passages along which the path continued. Clara was able to see pieces of moonlight scattered on the ground ahead where the

land became a steep slope rising four hundred feet to the head of the
hollow. It was at the summit where Bear Creek bubbled out of the leafy
earth, a crystal spring. She and Edward had discovered a cave there
under a giant rock. Clara hoped that would be the place where the kids
had taken shelter.

She moved up the precipitous path like a silent shadow stopping
now and then to listen. As she progressed, unseen things skittered off
the trail into the leaf duff or hunkered down into the tangle of brush.
Near the summit, Clara's heart clenched when a whitetail reared up,
snorted a sharp bleat of warning, and bounded through the thick laurel.

She approached the cave cautiously. The immense rock glowed in
the bright moonlight. At its base the cave was a dark throat. It was here
that Clara and Edward had found three abandoned coyote pups, which
they reared and then set free. It was here where the two returned often
to camp and make 'wilderness love', Edward called it, among the
conversations of tree frogs and the flutterings of bat wings. Many fine
memories were stored in this place.

Clara, rifle ready, safety off, stalked cat-like toward the entrance.
She moved from shadow to shadow careful not to crack a twig or allow
a branch to snap. She peered into the dark mouth straining her eyes for
movement, her ears for the sound of breathing. Nothing. Empty.

The roof of the cave was scorched black from the many
campfires she and Edward had built. The circle of stones was still in
tact. Clara lit a match. The floor was strewn with bat guano and small
bones of prey animals. The coyotes must have moved back here for a
while, she thought. The match burned out. Clara sat in the dark for
some time. She watched a great gray owl glide past the cave
noiselessly, a ghostly vision. "I wish I had your ears, owl," she
whispered. "April, Philip, where are you guys?" Clara lit several more
matches. She could tell that the ground had been disturbed, but
everything was such a jumble, it was impossible to tell whether the
tracks were animal or human.

In her mind Clara pictured the sprawling hump of the mountain
lying like a sleeping bear in the silver wash of the moon. She searched
the scars along its back, old logging roads that skirted the eastern ridge
all the way to the head of Fisk Hollow. She swooped over swamps and
ponds on the flat and glided through great stands of pines and around
glacial rubble, boulders spilled on the hilltop forming caverns and pits
large enough for children to fall through.

Clara was remembering the terrain, formulating a plan of places to
search, rocks to look under. Maybe the diver had already found them,
maybe not, she thought. Clara clicked the safety on the rifle, shouldered

it and headed east toward the logging road. No trail here. She kept the moon over her right shoulder to avoid walking in circles.

Invisible branches clawed at her face. Mosquitoes chewed on her neck and hands until she smeared them with mud. As careful as Clara was, she still tripped over roots and stumbled on rocks. An hour passed before she reached the logging trail. Still no sign of daylight, no sign of the kids. The going was easier here, and Clara felt if they were heading north, they would use this path.

The first sign of the two kids came where a spring had overflowed the trail creating a wide stretch of oozing mud. By match light the sneaker tracks were clearly visible. Clara's stomach turned when she saw a third set of tracks. Bill Pearson had been right. Someone had these kids. He was a heavy man who sunk deep into the mud. Each of his hiking boots had different tread. Clara touched the track as if it might tell her something about the man. The sides of the tracks had not caved in nor were they dried and hard like old ones. So that's it, she thought, they're traveling by night, hiding by day. Edward, this is not good.

Further on, Clara found what looked in the dim light to be the sleeve of a red tee shirt, but proved to be drenched in blood. It was still sticky. Clara held her rifle ready, finger on the safety and moved slowly down the shadowy trail.

Come daylight she knew they would hole up in the rock caves near the swamp or, if they were beyond that, the pine thicket on the bluff overlooking Fisk Hollow. The moon melted down into Sartwell Creek, a candle going out. The darkness doubled. Clara's eyes grew wide, her hearing more acute. She was an animal in search of prey. She remembered now that Edward had told her that if she ever needed to use a gun on a man, she should think of him as an animal, a creature that would tear her apart if she didn't do what needed to be done.

Clara searched the rock caves near the swamp. Nothing. No signs. Fresher tracks were found heading north. She was catching up. One track contained a pool of blood. She moved on.

A whitetail deer bounded across the trail as if it were being chased by dogs. Clara froze and listened to it crash through brush until silence returned. A half dozen mourning doves whirred through the dark, their wings whistling. The deer and the birds had been spooked out of their hiding places in the pine thicket.

With each step, Clara halted and listened. Step and listen. Step. She heard noises, a clanking, a deep voice, rough and angry. What was he saying? She moved in closer, turned off the trail into the pines. Someone was crying.

"Shut up, whore! I'll not have any woman of mine sniveling like a baby!" The stone ground words came through the dark like growls. Some bear talking to himself. The whimpering stopped.

A spark of light appeared amongst the thick, dead wood protruding from the lower part of each pine. The light grew to a yellow intensity slightly flickering. Clara heard the globe of the kerosene lantern creak into place. She heard the girl cry out, "No! No! Don't! You already killed my brother! Leave me alone!"

"He ain't dead, he's just sleepin'. And I'll do what I've a mind to with my pretty little woman."

Clara could plainly see the grim scene unfolding in the clearing. Two oaks had grown up amongst the pines creating with their canopy a kind of cave. The lantern set on a rock near where Philip lay face down, still as a corpse, his back covered with a dark stain. By one of the oaks next to him was a frame pack with a rolled sleeping bag attached.

The man moved like an animal, jean clad bowed legs, black hair dangled over the collar of his camouflage jacket in sweaty strings, large feet sheathed in one black, one brown boot. He had tied April to the other oak tree. Clara watched as he drew out his hunting knife and began cutting her clothes away. Clara could not see the girl. She saw the man's arms move, saw the torn blouse tossed aside, the bra land on a pine branch. She heard April cry out in protest. The man smacked her and lowered his head.

Clara could see now the terrified face of the young girl who looked as if she were being mauled by a crazed animal. Help me here, Edward, Clara thought. Stay with me. Steady this gun.

The girl was in the line of fire. Clara felt the ground and found a thick stick which she tossed over by the boy. The man whirled around at the sudden sound. He picked up the .22 rifle and fired into the brush. Worked the bolt and fired again. The thin pops had no echo, sounded like striking a wooden box. Clara could see his bearded face plainly. Skin the color of slugs. He stepped toward the boy and stood listening. April's head hung down, her breasts shown in the yellow light like small birds. Her yellow shorts were unzipped.

Clara threw a second stick in the opposite direction. The man whirled around and fired four more shots into the brush. "Goddamn 'coons!" he yelled. "Git the hell outta here! Shouldn't be interruptin' me and my wo..."

The man did not finish the sentence. Clara stood, aimed and fired. The explosion created an avalanche of thunder that rumbled into the valley. His head jerked. The man's hand went up to where his ear should have been. He crumpled like a falling elm tree.

Clara slung off her pack, removed the skinning knife and went to the girl. April held onto Clara sobbing and gasping for air, the stuttered breathing that comes with heavy crying. Clara helped her get on her torn blouse and tied it with a leather bootlace all the while whispering, "You're okay now. You're safe now. It's all over."

"Let me check on your brother," she said quietly. Clara stopped next to the dead man and pulled his jacket over his ruined head. She gently rolled Philip over. His shirt was a mass of blood.

April sighed, "He shot him this morning when Philip tried to pull him off me."

"He's alive, April, just barely. The bullet went all the way through, but he's lost a lot of blood. You're going to have to pull yourself together now so we can help your brother. You need to be absolutely strong until we get him down off the mountain. Okay?"

"Okay," she sniffed.

"Hand me my bag," Clara said. She dressed the wound, found a flannel shirt in the dead man's bag for Philip, cut stretcher poles and lashed green cross sticks to the poles with rope. April unrolled the dead man's sleeping bag onto the stretcher. Carefully, they slid Philip into the bag, zipped him in and lashed him to the carrier so that he would not roll out if they stumbled. Finally, Clara went through the pockets of the frame pack. She found a wallet with last year's hunting license in it.

Clara said, "Only identification is this old license. The name's been blotted out. I think we're ready to go. Listen, this logging trail leads right into Fisk Hollow. Old Man Rew has a place there. No phone, but he's got a truck. We'll send him for help. Can't be more than a few miles or so." She hugged the trembling girl.

"What about him?" April asked pointing to the lifeless body with no name.

"Well, if we don't tell anyone where he is then the animals will take care of him. He deserves that!" she said. "But I guess we should tell the warden approximately where he is. We needn't be too exact. They'll find him eventually." The girl almost smiled.

Clara grabbed the lantern and lifted the front of the stretcher. April lifted the rear. The two headed slowly out to the trail. Clara thought of Edward and began to hum to herself some wordless song that he had taught her. Across the hollow to the east, a gray smudge of light bled onto the night sky, and the darkness all around began its surrender.

Mina

1

The dilapidated Chevy truck rattled up Clara Hill's gravel road. It came to a halt in a cloud of dust brown as the truck itself. Jay Abbey slid out of the cab just as Clara emerged from the cabin door. She wore faded, blue denim bib overalls with the legs cut off just above the knee. Jay wore dark blue work pants with the legs stuffed into a pair of high top leather boots, which showed considerable wear. His work shirt was heavily soiled with 'Jay' stitched above the left pocket.

"Mornin', Miss Clara," Jay said.

"Hi, Jay," Clara said. "What are you doing way out here? Are you lost again?"

"Oh, no, not at all. I come with a birthday present fer ya from Saul. Said he couldn't remember the exact day but supposed this was the right week." Jay smiled and pulled off his gray Feed Mill cap exposing a thin mat of white hair.

"Well, it's the right week, just the wrong month. I was born in October, not August." Clara smiled.

Jay looked at the truck then at Clara. "Should I bring it back in October? It's all paid for in full."

"What is it?" Clara stood on her tiptoes trying to peer into the truck bed. Curly and Spike, the old hounds, began to whine from their run near the waterfalls.

"A washing machine! It ain't new, but works real good." Jay beamed.

"If that brother-in-law of mine can't convince me to move to town, he's determined to bring town to me. He knows full well I don't have electric or plumbing. He wants me to become civilized like those town folks who couldn't skin a rabbit if their life depended on it!"

"You want I should take it back?"

"Oh, no. A gift is a gift. You never know, Jay, when Saul might give me something useful. So let's just put it over there under the apple tree."

Jay looked perplexed. He ran his fingers through his hair, thumbed his suspenders a few times, put his cap back on and climbed up into the truck bed. The white enamel machine was strapped to a dolly. Jay eased it down from the tailgate and rolled it to the apple tree.

"Perfect," said Clara. "It's a top loader, too. You tell Saul thank you for the planter. Should look good with wildflowers and some leafy vines flowing down the sides."

"You sure you don't want it inside, Miss Clara?"

"It's fine right there. No room in the cabin anyway. Too full of junk...traps, snowshoes, rifles, skis, knives, you know, useful stuff." Clara smiled.

Jay still looked confused as he climbed into the truck and backed down the drive raising a fresh cloud of dust some of which landed on the white enameled machine.

———————

The morning was getting on. Clara fed the dogs chunks of fish and rabbit. She swept the cabin floors, cleaned the soot from the lantern globes, washed the breakfast dishes and brought in a load of wood for the cook stove. She collected buckets of water from the pond above the dam that Edward had built. Even though he had been gone ten years, she still talked out loud to him as if he were working right along side of her.

You know, Edward, this washing machine business is a real joke. Why can't your brother leave well enough alone? Next thing you know he'll be wanting me to buy soap rather than use what I make myself. Why in town they have one kind of soap for clothes, another kind for dishes and still another for bathing. What silliness! Dirt doesn't know the difference. Besides, all that store bought stuff makes you soft, makes you dependent. I don't intend to be neither.

People look at me, Edward, and say I'm poor, but poor ain't a choice, and I choose this place. It keeps your senses awake, keeps you tuned into natural time, not clock time. Edward, do you realize I don't even know what day it is. I know it's August, maybe the second week. I wonder if I'll know when my birthday comes.

Clara continued talking to Edward as she prepared her mid-day meal over an open fire near the elm stump. On a cast iron griddle she placed strips of venison tender loin. She mixed flour, water, diced onion and garlic into dough, which was placed in large clumps next to the sizzling meat. She put a tin box over the dough to act as an oven. Blue wood smoke curled about the griddle, perfumed the air with its incense and rose in a straight column into the blue of the summer sky. *It is a comfortable day*, Clara said to Edward as she poked the fire with a bent stick.

After eating, Clara walked to the lower field through which Bear Creek ran. She began her gardening as she did every day by repairing the fence, which nightly the deer attempted to undo. She hoed between the pole beans and the tomato plants. She checked the melons and lettuce, dug some radishes and frowned at the short stalks of corn. Doesn't look good this year, she thought. From yellow squash leaves, Clara plucked a few Japanese beetles and flicked them over the fence. "There's plenty for you guys to eat out there," she said aloud.

A car horn sounded from the main road along Sartwell Creek. An old Ford station wagon, which Clara recognized, turned up her road. It was Marsha Langstrom from Bakers Hollow over on Fishing Creek. Marsha was deep into her forties, a large, strong woman with a round, shining face. Her blonde hair had streaks of gray, but was mostly covered with a blue bandanna tied in the back.

Clara waved. She saw that Marsha was not alone.

Marsha pulled up to the garden, shut down the engine and got out of the car. "Hey, Clara! How ya doin' anyway? Haven't seen you since a while back."

"Doing just fine, Marsha, although I might have more success raising deer than vegetables. How about yourself?"

"Well, I've seen better days. That bunch a kids of mine been runnin' me ragged. Some days I feel twice my age. Told Mr. Langstrom we shoulda stopped at five but we went four over. The youngest, named after you, of course, is more trouble than the other eight put together!"

"Living up to her name she is! How is old Al coping?"

"He's beside hisself trying to keep all those mouths fed. The oldest are growd enough to help some which is a mixed blessin', They're all out hayin' today. Brought someone over I want you to meet."

Marsha gestured to the young girl in the front seat.

"Come on, Lily, git yourself outta the car. Thata girl. This here is Clara Hill, the lady I was tellin' you about. She's the one saved those Larkin kids years back. Clara is one of the finest people I know."

"Hello, Lily," Clara said extending her hand.

Lily looked at the ground. She did not shake hands. She was a beauty, Clara thought. Her long, blonde hair slid over her shoulders like corn silk just before it goes ripe. The strong afternoon light made her face pale. Her chin and cheeks were rounded, smooth as worn stone. Her eyes were blue-green. Depending on the light, they were like the underside of a leaf when storm winds blew or like deep pools of Bear Creek water reflecting a piece of sky. No matter the hue, Lily's eyes held an obvious sadness. She wore jeans and a light blue blouse printed with tiny white flowers. Her hands were clasped in front of her. Clara thought she carried herself like a clenched fist.

"Don't mind her none, Clara," Marsha said. "She's just a bit shy. Didn't get that from our side of the family. Lily's my niece, my sister's girl. You remember that Celie passed last winter. She had her a cancer. Celie always was frail, but she was a beauty just like Lily here. Celie got the looks and I got the brains is what Ma always told us. Lily got both. Smart as a whip she is. She even has book learnin', too. Can read and write. She got honor grades over there in Bradford."

Marsha put her arm around Lily and pulled her close. "So, Clara, do you think we could go up to the house and talk a bit? There's a favor I need to be askin'."

Clara thought she could sense underlying Marsha's words a thin veneer of urgency. "Of course, we can. And, Lily, you come up and meet my dogs. They love company."

Lily sat on the elm stump petting the dogs that whined and licked her hands. Inside the cabin Marsha explained about Lily. "Clara, this child has had a real hard time of it. Her mother's dead; her father ran off in the spring. They found his car up in the woods near Kinzua. The authorities figure he drowned hisself in the Allegheny. They dragged the river but never found no body. I didn't like the guy from the first. He just wasn't from around here. Celie liked him though. They never visited. To me that's evidence enough that somethin' ain't right. Lily managed to get herself pregnant about a year ago. The baby weighed less than a squirrel when it was born last winter. It only lasted a month. Died a few weeks before Celie did."

Clara poured some water into two mason jars. "Weak things don't live long in this world," she said. "It's the same in the woods as it is for people. It was probably for the best."

"I think you're right. So by fifteen, Lily has lost her baby, lost her mother and lost her father. Then she was took in by a neighbor lady who was one of these religious types. She locked Lily in her room nights trying to save her from boys. That only lasted to early May when Lily run off. The lady sent us a letter saying that Lilly was gone and 'good riddance to white trash' she said right in the letter. I try to think the best of people, but there are some fools in this world and she was one. I hope she does better in the next life!

"Mr. Langstrom got up a search party. They combed the area around Bradford on foot and horseback. Looked nigh on two weeks for that girl. Not a sign of her until a week ago when a trapper found her living in his line camp, a shack up on the plateau where all them beaver ponds is."

"She looks like she came through it okay," said Clara.

"She cleans up good. Lily was a mess when we picked her up at the county jail. They should've took her to the hospital. She was filthy, starving, all scratched up and bee bit."

"So," Clara said looking out the window at Lily and the dogs who had fallen asleep at her feet, "about this favor you need?" Clara already knew what it was; she could see the situation plain.

Marsha twisted her fingers together and said, "You know how it is with Mr. Langstrom and me and all them kids. It's like a tribe a Indians. We live in hand-me-downs and eat a lot a potatoes and beans. They just ain't nuthin' to spare. Mr. Langstrom says we can't keep Lily. She'd be the straw that breaks his back is what he says."

Clara sipped her water and smiled. "I'll make it easy for you, Marsha. How about you do me a favor and let Lily stay with me. This isn't a prize place for her to land. We could see how it works out. She may decide to run off again. But then you never know. She might just take to this rough living, this scratch in the dirt independence I got here."

Marsha hugged Clara. "I ain't got enough words to be thankin' ya, Clara. She's a good girl; she's just real hurt. Lily hasn't spoke a single word since I picked her up. All this hardship has kicked the spirit outta her. She's like one of them injured animals yer always lookin' after 'cept her's is inside where you can't see it."

"Does Lily know why she's here?" Clara asked.

"I explained how it was, but she didn't say anything."

"Well, let's go out and see what she thinks. Maybe we can get her to nod yes!"

The campfire near the stump was hot coals from which curled strings of blue smoke. A wind had come up and set the leaves of the surrounding woods to flapping; they whispered among themselves as if something was up.

Lily looked up, her sad face a beautiful flower.

Clara spoke, "Lily, your Aunt has asked if it would be okay for you to come stay with me. I've agreed as long as you say it's fine with you. I don't intend to mother you none. No one can take Celie's place. I can give you a safe place to be. The way it would be here is just two friends living together. We'll share in the work and the play. Each be respectful of the other's needs. You could come and go as you please as long as you don't make me worry. And I'll do my best not to worry you. Does that sound like a deal?"

Marsha said, "Our place, Lily, is just over the hill there. You can hike to the farm for a visit anytime."

"One other thing you should know," Clara said. "I talk out loud to myself all the time. Actually, I talk to Edward. You'll learn more about him as time goes on. Just didn't want you to think you were living with a crazy woman." Clara rolled her eyes.

Lily looked at the ground, the sky, then back at Clara. She nodded yes.

———————

Clara woke at two a. m. This usually happened when the dogs would bark at a porcupine or bear that had wondered into the door yard in search of food. This time, however, the dogs hadn't barked. The sounds that had disturbed her sleep had come from the front room where Lily was asleep on a cot. Clara listened in the dark. She could see points of starlight undulating to the contours of the hill outside her window. Deep moans followed by high, distressful cries came through the slat bedroom door. Clara lit the kerosene lamp and peered into the room.

Lily lay asleep on her cot near the kitchen sink. Her knees were drawn up tight to her chest, her face clenched. She sobbed, "No! No! No!" over and over again. After a few long minutes she was quiet, her breathing deep and regular. Clara put the lantern on the dinner table, picked up the quilt that had tumbled to the floor and covered the young girl.

Back in her own bed Clara spoke to Edward, I've *cared for shot bears, broken legged deer, poisoned birds and that coyote who chewed off his trapped leg, but I don't know about this, Edward. This girl is hurt bad, but it's not where you can get at it. I guess animals are that way, too. They get all nervous and scared and tied up inside when things in their world fall apart. I'll do what I can for her. We'll just have to see; we'll just have to see...*

Clara fell into a deep sleep. Her own anxieties played themselves out in dreams. In her last dream she was deep in the woods hiking near the source of Bear Creek. The sun had settled over Liberty Hill. The sharp shadows had dispersed. The twilight seemed to emanate from the trees themselves, from the dark leaves of the laurel bushes, from the gray-white rocks covered with silver lichen.

She was sitting on a log near the cave where she and Edward had so often made 'wilderness love'. From a great distance somewhere along the ridge came a lonesome whimpering, a child's cry. Clara followed the sound pushing aside the stiff laurel and the spidery ferns. Snorting an alarm before bolting off through the dense cover was a whitetail deer. Clara heard the calls for help again, much closer than before. At the edge of a small swamp she found the young girl. Her leg was caught in a bear trap whose teeth dripped blood. Matted in her hair were dead leaves and scraps of moss. Her shorts and blouse were torn and soiled. The girl's face was as bright as a flower glazed with rainwater. Clara unset the trap and gathered the girl up in her arms. She spoke to her softly as they headed down the creek path toward the cabin. "It will be okay," she whispered. "Everything will be fine now."

The girl whimpered.

———————

Clara awoke to the smell of pancakes. She found Lily in the kitchen dressed in jeans, a blue and white plaid shirt, and her hair tied with a blue ribbon. She had flour on her nose. The plank table was set with clay plates fired with a brown glaze, mugs of water, flatware and two bandanna napkins. Lily smiled at Clara.

"You can cook?" Clara said.

"Mmmhmmm," said Lily.

Clara thought to herself, almost a word.

The two ate pancakes while Clara talked. "I'm just not used to sleeping this late. The sun beat me up today. Last night I had so many strange dreams. Hope I didn't keep you up by chattering away in my sleep. Edward always said that I talked more at night than I did during the day."

She paused, took a forkful of pancake dripping with syrup. "So I've decided that today will be a kind of holiday, only the necessary chores, then we'll go for a hike up Bear Creek. I'll tell you all about Edward, give you my whole life story if you have the stamina to listen."

Lily cleared away the dishes and washed them in the wooden bucket of water she had brought in from the pond. Clara noticed that the cot was already folded in the corner and the bedding rolled up and stored on the cane bottom chair. Through the window she could see the clothes Lily wore yesterday hanging from the line. *All good signs*, she whispered to Edward.

When Clara returned from feeding the dogs and chickens, Lily was standing by the window holding a kestrel carved from dark wood rubbed to a matte sheen. Her fingers traced the delicate feathers of the small raptor.

Clara said, "That was my first attempt at carving. Originally I had planned to make dyes to get the colors just right because these little guys are so beautifully painted with black, rust and slate blue. But the berries I was working with just weren't quite on the mark. Then I remembered something Edward had told me about the stories he read. He said he thought the best ones left something to the imagination, the writer allowed part of the story to occur in the mind of the reader. So I just adopted that philosophy for my carving.

"Most afternoons you'll see at least one of these little birds fluttering above the field near the garden looking for insects, nice tasty grasshoppers. After you've seen one, you'll always have those colors in your head. I've been trying to think of a welcome present to give you. I think you've found it. So that one is yours, besides I have all these others. The red tail I did last year. The bobcat was real tough; it took near six months. The eyes were the hardest; they're so intense, a real look of the wild."

Clara pointed out other pieces that stood on shelves, rafters and windowsills. There were coiled snakes, an alert chipmunk, a dozen different birds including in one corner a Great Blue heron, one foot raised slightly, head and neck cocked as if ready to strike at an invisible fish.

She said, "What do you say we take a walk up to the ridge. There's something I'd like to show you. Let me throw a few things in a sack and we'll be ready."

Lily nodded.

2

L ily followed Clara past the waterfall, the pond and into the
woods. With each step she watched Clara's long, brown braid
slap from one side of the green canvas pack to the other. Curly and
Spike no longer barked when Clara left, but they watched intently as
the pair disappeared up the trail. Drifting wood smoke from the
kitchen stove perfumed the air. Panicked calls of blue jays tumbled
down the hillside. A raven, perched in the dark green shade of a
pine, watched them pass. The blue skin of the sky appeared to be
water with green leaves floating on its surface. The circular flight of
a hawk was reflected there. Deep in the still, blue water was the pale
stone of the moon worn smooth by endless motion. The hikers heard
the ceaseless gossip of the stream as they climbed higher up Bear
Creek.

Clara chose not to speak. Instead she pointed to those things she
wanted Lily to see. She put her face close to the emerald moss on a
rock and breathed deeply. Lily did the same. She pointed at a deep pool
where a pair of native speckled trout lay motionless, still as stones.
Clara showed her the large, square holes, one above the other, made in
a birch tree trunk by pileated woodpeckers. Where the path passed
under a towering white pine, Clara picked up what appeared to be a

large pussy willow bud. She broke it open in front of Lily revealing an assortment of tiny bones including a small skull and a foot.

Once they reached the summit, Clara broke the long silence. "This is what I wanted you to see, Lily."

She led her into a large cave at the base of a gray boulder the size of a house. Lily ran her fingers over the irregular rock wall tracing the depressions and bulges. Black soot coated the ceiling. Even though the air smelled of damp decay, the place had the secure feel of a solid shelter. The dirt floor was strewn with animal bones and dead leaves. A circle of stones was arranged in the center near the mouth of the cave. In it were three charred logs.

"The fire ring belongs to Edward and me. The bones don't. It seems the coyotes use this as a den every three or four years. They must have other hideouts north of here in the boulders. The bones belong to them or rather their prey. Let's see, we have a 'possum right here; there's a raccoon; this is a squirrel and that is a deer leg. And these, hmmm, seem to be dog or coyote. Not enough left to really tell.

"So I thought we'd build ourselves a little campfire and I could tell you all about Edward and this place. The crackle of a fire and the smell of wood smoke make for better storytelling I think."

Firewood was gathered, stacked in a teepee shape over dead leaves and lit. The blue smoke hit the ceiling and curled before slipping out of the cave and up the face of the great rock. Bones were swept aside and a gray wool blanket laid by the fire. The two sat on the blanket and were quiet for a long time. The yellow fire snapped and hissed as flames strengthened and fluttered through the dead wood. Clara offered Lily a jar of cool water. She took a long drink with her head tilted back. Clara drank as well and placed the jar back in the pack.

"It's always been hard for me to talk about Edward," Clara began. "He was such a sweet man, but strong in his own way. He liked to write poems and stories. Read everything he could get his hands on. I have a closet in the back of the cabin filled with his books. Whitman, Thoreau, Edgar Allen Poe, Yeats, all those Romantic guys, Shelly and the rest. Cooper, Irving, Hawthorne, Melville. He liked Shakespeare, too. In the evenings he'd read aloud to me. I didn't understand all of it, but I sure could appreciate how much he was enjoying himself. Since he's been gone, I've read and reread all his books. He liked to memorize things as well. He'd recite whole scenes from a play taking on all the parts. You should have heard him do Juliet!"

Lily smiled.

"I never laughed so hard in my life. He wasn't even hurt by it; he laughed too. Sometimes when we worked together in the woods cutting firewood or gathering mushrooms or berries, I'd listen to him recite *The Highwayman* or *Annabel Lee* or some such poem. He said that doing that was a real comfort. Those words and the way they were arranged reminded him, he said, of ideals that were really important."

As she spoke, Clara looked from the fire to Lily from time to time. Each time Lily was watching her but then looked away.

"His own stories and poems were never shown to anyone but me. I actually thought they were pretty good, each one serious and light at the same time. His vocabulary was way beyond mine even though we both finished high school together. He was more of a reader. I preferred to read tracks in the snow. But I could usually get the gist of what he was getting at. His best pieces of writing were entries from his woods journals. Every day he'd write down what he saw. Edward used to say that it taught him how to see, forced him to notice details. Colors, odors, movement, shapes, light patterns, sounds. The more he wrote, the harder he'd look at things."

Lily picked up a stick and poked the fire. Her blonde ponytail lay across her shoulder and she held her knees against her chest with her left arm. Now she kept her eyes on the fire, but Clara knew she was listening. Clara looked beyond the fire out at the bright morning sunlight. The dense leaves of the forest were silver and still in the cool morning air. Although she could see neither, she could hear the hum of insects and the brief flutterings of bird wings.

"One entry I remember," she continued, "was written the year before he died. It described an August morning like this one when he was cutting firewood on the other side of Sartwell Creek up Beckwith Hollow. In his journal he wrote that he had an uneasy feeling that he was being watched. The old mare harnessed to the stone boat was shuffling its feet. Finally he found the 'voyeur' he called it in an old beechnut tree nearby. It was a cougar stretched out along one limb. Edward described the muscular shoulders and legs, the slightly heaving chest as it breathed, how the light changed along its body from rust to yellow to a mustard color depending on the lie of the fur. He wrote about the small head and that with his eyeglass he could see how the hairs spread up the face and around the eyes 'like water parting for rock'. He explained about the steady gaze of those unblinking eyes. Looking into those eyes, he wrote, was like seeing into the distant past, into a time when the big cats were more common.

"Often Edward would write how what he saw affected him. In that entry he simply said he knew from that point on he'd never be the same person he was when he had gotten up that morning. So much of what he wrote taught me to focus on where I was, to be awake and alert to the natural world. Many people seem to pass through life not seeing half of what's there. They're preoccupied with yesterday and tomorrow. That's why I tried to point out things to you, Lily, on the way up here. But you've been in the woods, had to survive there. You probably saw those things before I did."

Clara placed a few more sticks on the fire without looking at Lily. She studied the backs of her hands for a moment while listening to the flute song of a wood thrush drift up the hillside. Lily watched a small gray spider begin weaving a web near the ceiling entrance just out of the stream of the wood smoke.

"The reason," she began again, "this cave is so special is that this is where we often came to sleep on summer nights. Edward called it 'wilderness love' because we were making love where the coyotes mated. Such sweet memories. And they are sweet because my grief at losing him played itself out years ago. He's been gone over ten years now. Killed by a falling tree. I was with him when it happened. Right after that I didn't want to talk to anyone. Not a soul. And the dreams started, awful nightmares where I'd be running through the woods looking for Edward. Trees were falling all around me. I'd call out his name over and over. Finally he'd answer from far off. I would rush on to warn him, but I could never get there on time. There would be the loud crack of a splitting trunk, rifle shots as the guide ropes he had attached to the tree snapped and that awful shaking of the ground. I always woke up crying in the dark."

Clara waited and then went on.

"But then things changed. I guess that's when I started to talk out loud to Edward. It's been almost eight years since he visited me in a dream. He stood at the foot of my bed and said that everything would be all right, that I should remember that he was the one who died, not me. He said in that dream that my sorrow was like the reds and yellows under the green of the summer leaves, that even though others could not see it, it was there just under the surface at all times. He said I must let go. He was freeing me from my grief. It's rare now for me to have bad dreams.

"I like my life now. I'm very comfortable in it. I haven't met another man because I live so far from town. The only men I meet out here have bad teeth and smell like bears. So now, Lily, you know more about me than anyone. "

Clara turned away from the fire and looked at Lily. She was crying. For a long time Clara held Lily cradled in her arms, rocking back and forth. She spoke softly to her saying that it was important to cry; it was the body's way of getting rid of too much sadness and anger. It was a pressure valve, she told her, that burst when we tried to hold our hurt inside, keep it captive so that no one would know, not even ourselves until we found a safe place to let it go.

"This cave is such a place, Lily," Clara said. "Cry all day if you like, all day."

The heavy sobs continued. It was as if Lily could not catch her breath. She gasped for air and wept harder, she heaved and coughed and wept some more.

"That's it," Clara said, "let it all out. Deep wounds like the ones you must be carrying are like a poison inside. Crying sucks it out. There, there, it's okay. Everything will be all right. You're safe now."

Clara did not ask what was wrong; she did not pry. After a time Lily's sobs subsided. And when she was finally quieted, she spoke.

"He took me," she whispered over Clara's shoulder.

Her voice was a leaf, thin, transparent, a blade of grass trembling in the wind. Clara did not flinch or ask who *he* was.

"The baby I lost was his," she continued. "And good riddance to it 'cept it wasn't that little thing's fault. It was his fault. He said it was my duty because mama was so sick all the time."

Lily's voice was being honed sharp with anger.

"Papa said that when she got well again, he'd stop. But mama never got well. For near a year he forced me. Sometimes I think mama died so's she wouldn't have to hear my sobs anymore. He used to scream at her to get out of bed and she no more 'n eighty pounds, couldn't even walk or talk hardly. Then he'd get himself liquored up and come into my room."

Lily breathed deeply.

"I know you're not supposed to be happy when someone dies, but I said me such a prayer of thankfulness when I heard papa had drowned himself."

Lily began to cry again. Clara handed her a bandanna from the pack.

"You know what you said," Lily continued, "about nightmares? I have them every night. My door opens and he comes in like a big shadow. He makes me swear not to scream while he ties my hands to the bedposts. Then I can feel his hands under my nightgown, cold and wet they are, like rats crawling all over my body. Every dream is the same. I beg him to stop, but he doesn't. I can feel him holding my breasts but I can't scream because I don't want mama to hear. I can even feel him inside me and I'm so scared I can't breathe. Then I wake up, my whole body like a cramped muscle. The dreams are so real I think I can still smell his whisky breath in the room. "

Lily sighs, sits up and wipes her face with the blue bandanna. Her eyes are red; her cheeks are wet. Several strands of hair have come loose from her ponytail and are matted against her forehead.

"I know he's dead, been eaten by the fishes, but I can't get loose of the feelin' it's not true. I'm so afraid he's going to come back for me, break into my room one night, and it wont be a dream. If only they had found his body so I could have seen him dead. Then I'd know."

Lily looked straight at Clara.

"Please, Clara, don't ever tell anyone, no one else knows. I'm so ashamed, I feel so dirty."

Lily laid her head back down on Clara's shoulder and cried softly. Clara held her like a baby.

"Lily, you have absolutely no reason to be ashamed," Clara whispered stroking her hair. "You're the one who was hurt, the victim. Your father, Orin, should have been the one ashamed, but I doubt he was capable of it. Don't worry, I wont tell anyone. I'm really not sure what to tell you, Lily. I am glad you told me all this.

"What I do know is that you've been hurt as bad as any human being can be, and there's no poultice I could concoct from wild roots and mud to ease your pain. No one can fix that kind of hurt from the outside. You're the only one can do it. And whether you know it or not, you already started healing yourself by saying out loud what's caused all this sadness. And you have to keep that conversation going, but it doesn't have to be with me. Talk to your dreams, to your thinking whenever that pain surfaces. Just say to it, you're not going to hurt me anymore, you're not going to control me! That's all you have to say. And ever so gradually, Lily, you will get stronger and the hurt will get sick and die off. Before you know it you'll have room in your life for laughter again. That's when you'll know you have yourself back. And I'll do whatever I can, whatever I can."

Lily sat up, reached inside her pants pocket, pulled out a wrinkled photograph and handed it to Clara.

"This is mama," she said. "It's the only thing I own. I carry it with me all the time. It was taken before she got sick."

Clara studied the black and white image. Through the creases, Celie was beaming, a rare beauty with a glint in her eye.

Clara said, "She sure was beautiful. Looks more like your twin than your mother."

Lily looked at the smoky fire and whispered, "That's what papa always said."

The two sat by the fire for a long time. The flames died away, the coals breathed, and plumes of gray smoke curled about the mouth of the cave.

On their way down the hill, Clara rattled on about her life. She explained her need to be self-sufficient. She said that by living off the land her life was richer, she was more alive to the world, more awake than those lulled into comfort by civilization. This kind of living, she went on, wasn't easy.

"In fact, that was the whole point. Easy livin' kills the soul, Edward always said. He taught me how to forage for edible plants, to trap and shoot for meat. He taught me how to protect myself from bears, mountain lions of which there are exactly none left, and even man if need be. If you're agreeable, Lily, maybe that's where we'll begin."

3

During the days, weeks and months that followed, Lily learned to snare rabbits and squirrels, to make spruce tea, to create a salad from dandelions and plantain, to catch trout in a stick trap of her own making and to shoot the old side-loading 30-40 Craig rifle. With the latter she was able to hit a ripe tomato impaled on a sharp stick at fifty yards. Clara had said to her that it was a hunter's obligation to be a good shot so that the animal being taken would not suffer. She even taught Lily to give thanks for those beings that sacrificed their lives so that she could live.

"A sign of respect," Clara said, "the Native Americans knew, and we have to learn."

Woven among the sessions on survival were long hours spent in quiet talk among the trees, by the pond, in the garden, along the banks of Bear Creek. Under the great sky, clouded or clear, they made their hearts known to each other.

One afternoon as they walked through an open field Clara said, "Real sorrow doesn't have a chance against wildflowers, winter storms or stars."

Lily was beginning to smile.

Thanksgiving was the time of the hunt. Clara sensed that Lily was tense. She assured her that she would know what to do when the time came. It was still dark when the pair started up the path along Bear Creek. The air was still and frigid. Their breath hung there in misty puffs. Their footsteps were muffled by the light snow of the previous day. Above, the stars were distant, minuscule specs of light, shimmering jewels strewn across the black of deep space.

"Edward used to say," Clara whispered, "the stars are a record of all the stories that ever played themselves out here on earth. See that cluster there above Leman Hollow?"

Lily squinted, "Yes."

"That's the whitetail you're going to get this morning. And just north there toward Beckwith, that string of bright stars is you lying in wait."

Lily said, "Do you see papa up there? I could shoot him right from here."

"I'm afraid he's drowned in the Milky Way. Better not shoot. You don't want to hit an innocent star."

The pair had scouted the deer trails that led up over the hill from Sartwell Creek. The deer spent nights along the creek drinking and feeding on the last of the sweet grasses. Come daylight they'd head for the deep woods to bed down. Clara claimed a spot at the base of a white pine, which offered a clear view of the run where it leveled off near the top of the hill. Lily sat down hill from Clara amongst a group of boulders. Clara knew Lilly's line of sight down the hill would give her first choice of the deer heading up.

The rifle was heavy across Lily's lap. Several times she checked to see that it was loaded, four copper cartridges with hollow-point lead in reserve and one in the chamber. She clicked the safety several times and tried to relax. Lily was warm in the long johns she had made for herself over which she wore denim jeans, a red checked wool shirt, high leather boots her Aunt Marsha had given her, and a blue cap knitted by Clara.

The first light began like a stain on the new snow and grew gradually among the leafless branches overhead. The air stirred slightly rattling a few dead leaves clinging to oak trees behind her. A titmouse whistled down by the creek and a chickadee flitted noiselessly among the rocks where Lily slept. She was curled against the lichen-covered rocks as if they were feather pillows. Her bad dream was back. The dark shadow that moved through doors made her face tense. The awful hands crawled through her sleep. She could not breathe. Lily wanted to cry out but was paralyzed. She could feel herself squirm like a rabbit in a snare. *Oh, come sweet death,* she dreamed, *and free me from this open wound of a life.*

The sky was now a river of light, the woods glowed in the sun's clean rays. All was white and silver. Lily awoke with a start at the sound of a rifle shot, its echo still thundering down the valley. She stood at once and shouldered the gun, tense and ready. She eased the safety off.

Twenty yards away Lily could see the fresh tracks of deer that had passed by her while she slept. She blinked her eyes and waited scanning the length of the run, listening for hooves running, sniffing the air. All was quiet. Seventy yards down the trail in a thicket of leafless saplings, Lily focused on a horizontal line. Everything in nature grows up Clara had said. So if you see it otherwise either it fell over or it's an animal.

Except for that thin line whatever it was looked more like rock, snow, tree. What Lily did know was that deer have difficulty sensing danger unless it moves, cracks a twig, or is downwind. The light wind was in Lily's favor.

Lily was amazed at how calm she felt. She sighted along the barrel and waited. Her breathing eased. It was as if she were in another existence. Her history evaporated. Yesterday was gone and tomorrow would not come. There was only now, her, the snow, the trees, the silver sky, this horizontal line.

After many moments had passed, the deer stepped clear of the saplings exposing its gray-brown side, its large eyes and its small antlers. A young buck, Lily thought. It lowered its head as if to feed and then jerked it up to attention to see if the danger it suspected had moved. It hadn't. Lily recalled something Clara had said: all shots must be conscious acts. She calculated distance and, knowing the lead would drop slightly, aimed at the spine just behind the shoulder. She fired.

The recoil knocked her back a step like it always did. The report avalanched down the valley like a receding storm. At first the deer looked startled. Then its forefeet collapsed so that it knelt as if taking a bow, blood pumping from the hole behind the front shoulder. The hind legs gave way. It looked at Lily, its feet pawing at snow and dead leaves. Finally the deer lowered its head, closed its eyes and lay still.

Lily suddenly felt lightheaded. She sat down, clicked on the safety and leaned the rifle against a rock. She was holding her head in her hands when Clara came running down the path, her single braid leaping wildly.

"You okay," Clara said leaning her own rifle against a tree. "I've missed before, too. Don't worry; there are other days and besides we still have the one I shot."

Lily sat up quickly wiping tears from her eyes. "Missed? I didn't miss! I shot him right through the heart. He never had a chance. In fact, I felt as though he didn't want another chance. He's just down there by the thicket. He's not too big though."

"Way to go! The smaller ones are better eating anyway. How'd that big one I got ever get by you?"

"I'm afraid I fell asleep. I was having an awful dream when I heard your shot. I waited like you said to see if any deer would circle back to me. That's when I saw this one. I felt so calm, Clara, when I fired, but now I'm shivering all over."

They walked down the path to where the buck lay in the snow. Lily kneeled next to him and petted the soft brown and white fur of his neck. She closed his eyes the way you would for an old aunt who has just died. Sitting there next to the growing red stain in the snow, she asked that its strength become a part of her and thanked it for its life.

Clara watched and then said, "Lily, now that the easy part is over, we begin the hard work. We have to field dress these deer and drag 'em out of here. I think we should start with yours. I'll guide you through. The main thing is not to rupture the glands right there on the inside of the legs. That musk scent'll ruin the meat."

Reluctantly Lily inserted her knife at the vent between the hind legs and drew it up the belly to the chest cavity. Steam rose from the fresh incision. Clara gave her a strong stick the color of bleached bone to hold the chest cavity open. She slid her hands in among the wet warmth of the organs to locate the heart and liver each of which she cut free and placed in a skin sack Clara had for that purpose.

"You know," Clara said, "if you're ever suffering from hypothermia out here in the woods, putting your hands and feet inside an animal could make the difference. Also, did I tell you that it's tradition going way back that with a first kill the hunter honors the deer by eating part of the liver raw. That is the surest way of transferring the life energy of the animal to you."

Lily looked at Clara, wiped her face with a bloody arm and said, "I think I'm going to be sick."

"That's the other tradition," said Clara.

Lily cut loose the rest of the viscera and spilled it out of the cavity onto the snow in a heap of bloody balloons and worms.

"Ravens and fox will feast tonight!" Clara said.

Lily used snow and dried leaves to clean some of the blood from her hands and arms. Clara showed her how to make a drag with two sapling poles and sticks lashed to them with wild grape vine so that it looked like a kind of rustic ladder. They tied the deer to the drag. Clara said, "Just one thing left to do, Lily. My deer!"

———————

The pair made their slow way down the creek path stopping often to rest. Each towed a travois behind them with deer, rifle and pack secured with vines. The strawberry snow and drag tracks told the tale of what had happened on the hill that morning. The snow was a reflector doubling the sunlight pouring through the leafless trees. Clara and Lily squinted as they made their way along Bear Creek. To Clara, the tumbling water was a song played on one of nature's instruments. That is how Edward described it. The wind was a bow drawn across the strings of the leafless trees. As she walked she remembered summer thunder, how lightning would fork from a cloud as black as a woodstove, the thunder song pour out of a hard cloud shaped like an anvil and crash about her shaking her bones with its rhythm. She was attuned to subtler music as well. Bird voices, frog choirs, and the long low hum of those myriad insects who take no breath between notes or rub legs or flutter wings with no caesura, nature's mantra, the great meditation of all things upon the one great mystery of which each is a singer. *Edward*, Clara said to herself.

Right now, though, only a few scattered bird sounds played along with Bear Creek as it coursed through the snowy woods. Clara wondered if they were calling to each other, singing to themselves to stave off the chill of loneliness, or if they were talking to some lost mate the way she talked to Edward. What sorrow do birds know, she thought.

Traipsing through the snow, Lily perspired heavily. Her thoughts for once were clear, not tainted with the constant babble of old wounds, the angry voices that always shouted, the movie in her head that demanded her attention and would not be shut off. She thought instead about the deer, both of them. How nature wrings life out of death, a simple cycle: clean, efficient, necessary. She felt, this morning, like a part of nature, the same as the raptor and squirrel, the fox and rabbit, and even going back into the distant past, the wolf and elk. She had felt this before in the spring when she lived alone out on the plateau foraging for food. It was harsher then; she was ill equipped for survival. Now, under Clara's tutelage, she had learned how to make do, and if she had to go into the wild again, she could do so.

Lily felt comfortable in her thoughts. Her idea of the wilderness reflected her view of life. She said to herself, school taught me some

fairy tale nature, an unreal portrait, storybook nature, nature as servant
to men, benevolent nature. She knew now that they were all lies or at
best half-truths. Real nature is brutal and beautiful, things being eaten
alive while pastel sunrises sweep across the sky. Nature doesn't serve
me, she thought, it is me. It isn't over there and me here, but rather I am
in it and it is in me. As metaphor to her own life, there was hardship
and cruelty. But ever so slowly Lily began to see clear moments of
beauty.

As she struggled along the path dragging the loaded litter she said
to herself, maybe that is what healing is, a balance between confidence
and doubt, joy and pain, beauty and sorrow, friendship and loneliness.
Before, Lily could not remember being a child. Between that distant
time and now, a kind of wall had been erected which made her feel as
though she had been born old. Names and faces of dolls were gone.
Games played on summer evenings with neighborhood kids were
erased. Dissolved were the holidays, red dresses and daydreams, those
long journeys of the imagination where hope grew like a flower whose
blossom opened to endless joy. Lily knew now that that was what
existed on the other side; over the long horizon of that opaque wall, her
lost joy lived.

"I can hear the falls," Clara shouted. "There's the cabin! Just a
little further."

Lily said, "Good thing."

4

The two dragged their burdens into the dooryard. At the head of the gravel drive parked near the washing machine planter was Saul's old pickup. The Ford hood ornament along with the grill had been staved in from hitting a deer in the spring which Saul field dressed right on Route 6 before bringing the carcass up to Clara.

"Hey there," Saul said appearing around the corner of the cabin.

His head was covered with a red knit cap. He had a kind, oval face with a dark beard peppered gray. Tan suspenders were stretched over the red and black plaid of his wool shirt and were attached to his canvas hunting pants. The pants were tucked into high-top leather boots that had seen plenty of wear.

"Hey to you," Clara said. "Sure glad you're here. We could use some help hanging these deer in the shed. Let 'em cure a bit before butchering. Saul, you remember meeting Lily a few weeks back."

"Sure do." Saul inspected Lily's deer and then her. "With that blood swiped across yer forehead, I'd say Clara here put you through one of those Indian rituals she's so partial to."

Lily smiled, a thing Saul had not seen on his last visit. He remembered how cold Lily had been toward him, which Clara called natural considering the troubles the girl had endured.

Clara scolded Curly and Spike who were sniffing the dead deer. They slunk back to their bare sleeping spots near the stump and watched.

Clara teased, "What brings you out this way on a week day? Don't you have a job anymore or did that glass plant finally discover how little you do?"

Saul grinned, "You know, Clara, they couldn't operate without me. I just took the day off to bring out a few supplies, visit with you and see if you hooked up that washer yet. Alls you have to do is give me the word and I'll plumb out the whole cabin so's you could have runnin' water inside. Kitchen sink, indoor toilet, washing machine, the works!"

"The problem I see with having the works," Clara said, "is that half the time it's just going to break down whereas if I don't have it, it's less likely to do so. What you could do is help us with these 'ungulates' as Edward used to call them."

Saul took hold of Lily's litter and dragged it around to the right of the cabin to the shed. Clara followed. He undid the hasp and opened the heavy, double slat doors. Birds fluttered and cooed in the rafters. Inside he threw two braided ropes over separate beams. Clara and Lily undid the vine bindings, removed their rifles and packs and tied one end of each rope around the antlers of their deer. Saul pulled the rope while the two women, hugging the stiff body of Lily's deer, lifted it, legs dangling, tongue lolling like a large, pink slug, eyes protruding in surprise, their flame extinguished, until it swung well off the ground like a hanged man. The chest cavity was still held open by sticks and the red rib cage had already started to turn black. They did the same with Clara's deer. Clara got several burlap potato sacks from a bin and placed them on the ground beneath each deer.

"That'll catch the blood drippings," she said. "We are going to eat well this winter, Lily. When it's time I'll teach you how to cut one of these up into steaks and tender loin and roasts. Then we'll tan the hides and make you a pair of slippers and a coat maybe."

Lily said, "I think I feel a little sick."

Saul went to his truck and removed several wood crates. One had boxes of shells for shotgun, rifle and pistol. "Thought you'd need all this to get your deer this year," he said, "but guess I was wrong. I think I got everything on your list."

"What list?" Clara said.

"The one you would have written if I'd remembered to ask."

Clara sorted through the other crates, which contained coffee, flour, sugar, skeins of colored yarn and bolts of cloth.

"Those was Molly's idea. She thought what with Lily being here you might want to make some things."

"I could really use these crates! How is she doing anyway?"

"Poor thing is run ragged by our boys. The three of 'em keep her on her toes. The youngest got a broken arm fallin' out of a tree house. Little Edward's got poison ivy all over and Saul, Jr.'s in love."

"He's only nine!"

"Not no more. He was nine last you saw him two years ago. But all my ancestors were early lovers. I known Molly since we was ten. Thirty years. She keeps saying she wants to trade me in on a new model, but I tell her straight out how disappointed she'd be 'cause they just don't make 'em like they used to!"

Lily laughed. "I'm going to wash up," she said, and walked over to the falls.

Saul said to Clara, "You think we could take a walk down along the creek?"

"Sure. I'll get Lily."

"I think we should do this alone, Clara."

Clara looked puzzled, then looked up to where Lily leaned near the spillway splashing water on her face. "Something has happened, hasn't it?"

"Yes."

"Lily," Clara called to her, "Saul and I are going for a short walk. When we get back, we'll cook up some food."

"Okay," Lily said.

———————

Saul and Clara followed Bear Creek beyond the snow-covered garden to where it crossed the field before joining Sartwell Creek. Puffs of white clouds drifted in the deep blue sky like smoke signals that warned of approaching danger, armies of trouble marching through the forest, unseen enemies preparing for battle. Yet the field blazed white in the brilliant sunlight, and the whispering creek talked of tranquility, a comforting song whose lyrics soothed the listeners. The contrast did not escape Clara's notice.

"So what is it then?" she asked hesitantly, twisting her long braid in her fingers.

"You know how it is in a small town, Clara, how everyone sort of knows everyone else's business. Well people know about Lily being out here and about her mama dying and her father drowning hisself and all. What they don't know is about her being abused. You said a while back as best you could tell her father done it, and if I was to hear anything, I should let you know right away. Well, I heard something. That's why I'm here."

Saul stroked his beard and shuffled his feet in the snow.

"Say it plain, Saul. I know you don't like carrying bad news. Did they find his body?"

"No, not at all. It's worse. Old Pete who spends most of his time on a bar stool ever since that young wife of his took off to Canada called me last night from the Butler House. He sounded sober enough. He asked what I knew about Lily. I said not much more than what he did. So he said a fella just left the taproom who was askin' a lot of questions. He wasn't from around here so according to Pete no one gave him a straight answer. Pete said he was a real rough lookin' character, a big man, black hair and a beard. No politeness in him. Skin was awful pale, scarred up some, face square as a block of wood. Pete said he had a considerable limp on him, almost draggin' his right leg. Told everyone at the bar he heard his daughter Lily was hiding out over here somewheres, and he would find her no matter what."

Clara felt sick. This news was like a disease returning. She could not speak. She just held her head and swayed back and forth. She looked up the creek toward the cabin but could not see Lily.

"Some of the guys at the bar told this guy that they heard she was up past Eldred near to Olean. Another said she left there and went to Buffalo or clear to Canada. But Pete didn't think he bought it. I saw the guy this morning on a bench in the Square right across from the state liquor store. Dressed all in black drinking something from a paper bag."

"That's sure enough him," Clara said. "Lily described him just the way you did. Her Aunt Marsha from over to Fishing Creek used that same phrase 'not from around here'. This is not good at all. Lily's been making real progress out here, Saul. Did you see that smile and hear her laugh? She's fought a hard battle just to get to that point. He hurt her as bad as any person can hurt another. He used to call her his bastard daughter because she had blonde hair not black like his. What can we do, Saul? We can't let him find out."

"I already had a talk with Sheriff Bates. Told him this guy seemed to be a dangerous sort and that he should keep an eye on him. Bates said he could do that best if the man was in jail so he was on his way to pick him up for vagrancy or something. He said he'd give him as much aggravation as was legal and maybe that would scare him off, cause him to clear out.

"I also talked with Tauscher, the judge. He said you should file papers today for legal custody of Lily; you would be her legal guardian.

She's of an age where she can choose he said. Then no one can take her away."

Clara looked at Saul. "The law won't stop him. He should be put away for what he did, but I don't think Lily is strong enough for that yet. This is going to erase any sense of safety she's gained. It'll scare her to death."

"You want I should move out here for just a bit to keep an eye on things?"

"No, Saul, I'll go into town with you and see the judge, then I'll come back and tell Lily and the two of us will figure what to do." Clara sighed.

"Judge said he'd be glad to come right out here. He needs to have Lily sign, too. Said he'd be out around sundown if that's okay with you."

Clara nodded.

They walked back to the cabin. Lily was playing in the snow with Curly and Spike. They vied with one another for her attention. As Clara and Saul approach, Lily looked up.

"Saul's heading on back to town. He'll be out again soon. He wants you to teach him how to hunt deer."

Lily waved good-bye. Saul backed down the gravel road. Clara brushed snow away from the stump and sat next to Lily.

5

Clara was surprised at how calmly Lily took the news. She sensed a dimming in the light of her eyes before Lily turned them to look at the ground, which was what held her gaze when she first arrived in Bear Creek. Clara also noticed a slight tensing of her cheek and neck, an almost imperceptible clench of the body, so subtle that Lily herself may not even have been aware of it. Clara had been ready for hysterics or weeping, some falling apart, a trembling fear springing from the reality that her dream serpent had resurrected its demon self. Clara was certain that all the horrific details of her nightmare life would flood back like ice in the veins paralyzing Lily in a catatonic state. For this she was prepared.

When Lily looked away from the ground and back at Clara, her eyes were hard marbles, a deeper blue, cold as creek stones. There were no tears welling up, nor any sign of fear in that soft rock face.

"Good," she said.

"What do you mean 'good'?" Clara said.

"I mean I knew he was alive. Because I know it, I can't be surprised. I am not who I was. When he comes for me, I'll be ready. There is no defenseless little girl here. She is dead. He killed her with bad dreams."

Her voice was calm and steady.

"For what it's worth we have the law on our side," said Clara. "But I don't think that will keep him away. Sheriff Bates will put him on the train for Olean or Buffalo. That's the direction everyone said you were headed. It won't take him long before he doubles back this way. I wonder if he paid your Aunt Marsha a visit."

Lily said, "I think she'd a been here by now if he had. Should I hike over there and warn her?"

"We'll both go. Safer these days to travel in pairs. I'll just throw a few things in a sack like Edward's Colts. We'll practice some along the way."

The trip over the hill to Baker Hollow had yielded little in the way of talk. Clara knew Lily needed to figure things and if she wanted advice she'd ask. At the farm, Lily sat alone on the porch while Clara explained to Marsha and Al. Finally she said, "That man did the devil's work on Lily. The details don't matter, but if he shows here, you mustn't let him know about my place. Steer him off north like everyone else."

Marsha reminded Clara that she never did think he was any good. "Something wrong with a family what won't visit; afraid of secrets gettin' out," she said.

Al offered to drive them back in the farm truck, but Clara said, "Walking the woods seems to help some. We have to get back now because the Judge is probably waiting on us."

Marsha held Lily. Lily said, "It'll be okay. Clara's taking good care of me."

On the hike back from Fishing Creek, the sun had emerged from behind dark storm clouds in the west and softened the snow. Across the trail down Bear Creek the shadows of trees lay like wet oak planks or slats of an old fence long ago trammeled flat. The air had warmed and both Lily and Clara wiped sweat from their foreheads.

Near the hilltop the pair practiced with Edward's pistols. Clara explained that one of the .45s had belonged to Edward's grandfather, the other to his father. Lily had the grandfather's gun with EH burned into the walnut handle. They held the revolvers with both hands, sighted along the barrels to a square pileated woodpecker's hole in a white pine twenty some yards off and emptied their six shots. The reports were hollow, flat cracks like wide boards falling square on a wood floor. Pine chips flipped away from the tree as lead penetrated the soft skin and cambium tissue. With each pull of the trigger, the cylinders turned. With each shot, the pistols reared up exhaling a plume of acrid smoke, which hung in the still air, a ragged little cloud.

The sun had fallen behind the endless mountains by the time they reached the cabin. Parked near the elm stump was Saul's truck behind which was the Judge's black Pontiac, a two tone blue with a patent leather shine. Protruding from the hood an amber likeness of the Chief.

The dogs barked Clara and Lily's arrival. Saul and the Judge emerged from the cabin door.

"Lily," said Saul, "this here is Judge Tauscher."

They shook hands.

"Now, Miss Lily, has Clara explained everything to you?" said the Judge.

"Yes."

"Do you agree that Miss Clara shall be your legal guardian until such time that you come of age?"

"Yes, sir."

"Your father Orin was in my court this morning. The way I explained things to him was that because there was ample suspicion of abuse, he wasn't to try to contact you as long as you were in McKean or Potter County. Beyond that I have no jurisdiction. However, I warned him that if he disregarded my order, I'd personally see to it that he'd spend the next very long time in our jail. He said he was headed north. Sheriff Bates put him on the 3:50 to Olean.

"Now, Lily, if yer willing to press charges, I'll have him picked up and brought back here. The judge up there is my cousin so it wouldn't be any trouble. But Saul says yer not wanting to do that, is that so?"

"Yes, sir. I just want him gone."

Lily's eyes were hard as rock, iris the color of lichen.

"So then if you two will step over here to my field office, I need you to sign a few papers."

They walked to Saul's truck. The judge spread the papers with the County insignia out on the hood and pointed to the marks on several sheets.

Lily signed.

As Clara signed she said, "Let's just say Orin comes back and finds us up here on Bear Creek."

"You let me know and I'll lock him up. If he threatens you, do what you have to do and we'll figure out the details later. A judge like myself isn't supposed to give that kind of advice, but like Saul says, you live way the hell out here in the middle of nowheres. Things are a little different. Besides I didn't like the look of that man. Rough character for sure. Kind of spooky, too, the way he drags that leg around."

Lily shuddered.

The Judge and Saul backed down the gravel road. The engine noise grew fainter and fainter until silence returned. Clara and Lily stood in the dooryard for a long time embracing one another. No words were exchanged.

———————

It was still early morning when Clara and Lily began skinning the two bucks. The north side of the shed was covered in neat rows with pairs of deer antlers. Lily asked, "Is this your trophy wall?"

"No, not at all. Edward never believed in sport hunting. He started putting those antlers up to honor the deer that gave their lives to us. He considered it a shrine. Some antlers we used to make tools or handles for things, but most of them are up there. I guess it's our way of showing respect. Outsiders think its gruesome, but it's not so when you live close to nature."

"Each pair of antlers is connected by a little piece of skull," said Lily.

"That way," said Clara, "you can get at the brains more easily. What we're going to do is make a brain paste to smear on the hide in order to tan it."

"I'm not going to like this, am I?" said Lily.

"Probably not because it's so gross, but you'll love the leggings or coat or vest you make. They make winter more bearable. Later we'll snare beaver or mink to make slippers. They have good fur. Hair stays in better. If we didn't remove the fur from these deer hides, they'd be shedding all over the place. There are lots of steps to this over several days, so why don't we get started. Come on in and I'll show you how to do everything on my deer, then you can do yours."

Clara got a stool from the stall. "I'm going to need this to reach everything," she said. "There's another one by the rakes. Use that. Just watch what I do, and then you do it."

Lily stood on her wobbly stool next to her deer gripping her hunting knife as if she might be attacked. She was pale and nervous.

"You know that holster for the .45 your wearin'?" said Clara, "I made that years ago. Reach behind you and feel how supple that is."

"If I reach anywhere, I'll fall on my head."

"Okay, follow me."

Clara sliced the skin scribing a circle around the foreleg just above the hoof. She did the same with the other three legs. She also slid the knife along the inside of each thigh and foreleg from the belly cut made for field dressing up to the circular incision. "On this next cut, Lily," Clara said, "make sure you don't go too deep."

Half way up the neck Clara sawed through the tough skin. Her blade moved quickly around the circumference of the neck and a final slice up the throat from the chest cavity.

"Make your cuts shallow. Just skin, not muscle and stuff. Good, Lily. Now the neck."

"I'd feel better if this thing weren't bigger than me. Feels like I'm skinning a human."

"I guess you'd use the same technique, but I don't think the final product would be as good. And if that deer was your size, it'd be a fawn. Try to think of something else while you're cutting 'cause this is the easy part. It gets worse. Now we put these knives away. Don't want to poke any unwanted holes. Here's a skinning stone. Bear Creek made both of these pieces of slate for us. It probably took the creek about a half million years to make them smooth and flat like that. Just peel the skin back like this, starting at the top. Push that stone in as if you're slicing with it. Work slowly, gently. Try not to let muscle or fat stick to the skin as you pull it away. That makes for more work later. Don't fall off that stool. You got it?"

"Yes, I think so."

Lily moved the stone along the clammy flesh pulling the skin with the other hand. Most places she just used her fist and fingers.

"It's just like takin' off a coat," said Clara.

"Not quite," said Lily. "Is there any way to put his tongue back in? It's just hanging there like a hunk of meat."

"Too late. Stiff as stone now. You could just cut it off."

"Never mind," Lily shuddered.

When they both finished, Clara took the two hides up to the pond, anchored them to a length of rope and threw them in.

"We'll let them soak 'til tomorrow. It'll loosen up the hair. For now, we need to do some butchering. Let's go back to the shed."

Inside, the two skinless bodies hung, their cavities dark red from dried blood, a thin sheath covering exposed muscle pocked with white fatty deposits. The translucent membrane revealed a mountainous roadmap of blue vessels pulled taut at certain intersections by stretched white tendons.

Clara handed Lily a hacksaw. "Run this over a flame a time or two to get it clean," she said. "Then you'll do the big cuts; I'll do the small."

Lily severed bone until the left haunch separated from her deer. She staggered with it to the butcher-block table Clara had just cleaned. She flopped it onto the table.

"I forgot to tell you, Lily, you have to cut off the feet first."

Clara smiled. Lily didn't.

"Gross," Lily said. She got the saw and cut grimacing as she did so as if the deer might still be alive. She removed the remaining seven feet and stacked them on a bench like cordwood.

While Lily continued quartering the deer, Clara divided the larger pieces into roasts, tender loin and steaks. Clara showed Lily how to skewer the smaller pieces on hooks in the drying room off the back of the shed. "Once they've dried properly, we'll put them out in the smokehouse. Whenever we're hungry, we grab a few slabs of venison, soak 'em for a half day or so to get the juice back in and cook 'em on a spit over our campfire or in a stew pot inside with mushrooms, peppers, some wild onion, carrots and potatoes. Mmmhmmm! Doesn't that sound good?"

Lily smiled weakly. She said, "My hands, face and body are covered with sticky ooze, blood and fat grease. I'm really not too hungry. Maybe in a few weeks when I recover."

"Recover? We just got the easy part done. Tomorrow and the next day will be the real test of character. I think you'll pass."

In the morning Clara taught Lily how to test the hide hair to see if it was loosening up. The fur let go with a light tug. "They're ready," Clara said.

They draped the first hide, fur side down, over a six-foot fleshing log, which was braced waist high at the tapered end and ankle high at the other end. The neck of the skin was at the high end. Clara showed Lily how to use a rib bone as a fleshing tool to scrape off fat and meat still attached to the skin. Using both hands, she slid the bone; curve down, along the pelt. Clara said, "If we were going to keep the fur on, we wouldn't have to do all this soaking and we'd be scraping from the other direction. We should be able to get both of these fleshed today."

Lily sat on a stool and watched Clara work. "Clara," Lily said. "I had such a vivid dream last night."

"Can you still remember it?"

"Oh, yes, every detail."

"Was it the nightmare?"

"No, well, yes. It started like the bad dream always begins, but just for a little while, then it changed. I was locked in my room. Someone was turning the key, turning the handle. Another door appeared at the other end of my room. It opened. I escaped into the forest. I wandered in the woods for days and days. There were great white pines towering like sentinels on guard. Their immense branches, thick as my arms, reached out to the next tree. I felt such happiness, such security. I climbed as near the top of one of the trees as I dared to look out over the mountains, which stretched one after the other clear to the horizon in every direction. When night came, I stayed in the tree and watched the stars. I even read a few of the stories they have to tell."

"Was your story among them?"

"In a way it was because they were about the people I know, and if I had my own story, those people would be in it. There was one about you and Aunt Marsha. There was one about mama, which wasn't sad at all. Then there was one sad one about papa, a very lonely star, his. I really wanted to be in that part of the dream so I could tell him how much he hurt me and ask him to go far away. But I wasn't.

"Too bad we're not the authors of our own dreams," Clara said. "But then maybe we are in a way. You were able to think of what you would say had the situation arose to allow some saying on your part. And you realized that even outside your dream, that probably isn't going to happen."

Clara stood erect and rubbed her back. Lily took her place and began fleshing out the lower part of the skin. She said, "I think I learned something else in that dream. That I'm not real afraid. I'll do what I can to avoid papa, but if that's not possible, it will be okay. I'm not afraid anymore and that's a good feeling. Why do you suppose, Clara, that's so?"

"I just think you uncovered your real self. Orin almost had you convinced that what happened was your fault, that you deserved it. But nothing could be further from the truth. You know that now. You just got yourself back."

"Yes, that's good, isn't it?"

"It is."

"Yes it is. And this here is really gross!" Lily pushed the rib bone along the hide scraping ahead of it a reddish white gelatinous roll. The road kill smell made her dizzy.

Clara said, "Tonight we soak these in the old galvanized tub. Hope it doesn't leak. To help the process along, I'll show you how to make my special concoction from wood ash. We pour that in the tub water with the skins. Then tomorrow we scrape and tan."

After breakfast Lily helped Clara build frames upon which to hang the hides. Small holes were cut around the perimeter of each skin. Clara used leather strips from previous deer to secure the hides to the frames.

Once the skins dried, the two used long handled, sharp scrapers, which Edward had made to remove the hair and cuticle layer of skin. Clara explained how she made glue from the cuticle shavings that were collected on a piece of burlap.

When both skins were scraped, Clara said, "Edward used to say that every animal has enough brains to tan its own hide. It's true, too. Brain tanning is a way to condition the hide. This is the part you won't like, Lily. Come on in the shed."

Clara showed Lily how to remove the antlers and the top part of the skull. "These will go on the antler wall later," she said.

Clara wore rubber gloves. She gave a pair to Lily who watched her scoop out the deer brains with her hand and dump the gray mass into a dented saucepan. "I don't think I can do this," she said.

Slowly Lily slid her hand inside the skull, exhumed the dense, gray mass, and plopped it into her own saucepan. Its consistency reminded her of the liver she had saved from field dressing the deer. The brown marble of the deer's eye watched her work.

"Good," said Clara. "Just don't ever let your boyfriend know you did this. They don't think it's very romantic."

"If I smell like these brains, I wont have to worry about ever having a boyfriend."

"Now comes the gross part. You may wish to hold your breath. Later we'll put these heads up in the woods for raccoon, fox and raven. They also make good winter homes for mice."

With saucepans in hand, the two walked out to the elm stump, past the whining dogs to the campfire. A frame made from several layers of chicken wire over the fire formed a grill.

Clara said, "We need to get these nice and hot, not boiling, but real warm. We pour them into these slat buckets and then mash them into a thick soup with those pestles I've laid out. Very gross. Make sure you wear those gloves. You don't want to get any of this goo on your own hide. It'll react to your skin the same as it does the deer's."

The wood smoke curled blue among the leafless trees. A woodpecker knocked on a hollow tree up on the side hill. While Lily mashed, Clara removed the skins from their frames and laid them on the butcher-block table. Together they rubbed some of the brain juice into both sides of the hides. Then the hides were immersed in the remaining soup and left there overnight.

The following day the skins were reattached to the frames, kneaded with old ax handles, and finally hung in the smokehouse over a fire made of punky wood. The thick white smoke drifted like fog up along Bear Creek. Clara noticed that it had been a while since Lily had made any mention of Orin.

6

Hours went by. Days passed. Weeks disappeared into months as the numb heart of winter hardened into a frozen crust over all the mountains and valleys. The sky was the color of old river ice, white-gray, with snow falling continuously. The woods grew silent; Bear Creek whispered and steamed in the crisp air. Occasionally a fox barked in the evening or at midday a woodpecker drummed on a dead tree somewhere up near the ridge.

Morning chores were executed in slow motion. Feeding chickens. Feeding dogs. Collecting eggs. Splitting wood. Filling the wood box in the kitchen next to the cook stove. Preparing venison, rabbit or squirrel stew. Once in a while roasting a turkey or duck. Potatoes, carrots, beans, mushrooms and peppers were always simmering amply spiced with onion and garlic. Sometimes dumplings floated like snowcapped islands in the brown broth. The strong odor permeated the cabin, defeated the frigid world that surrounded them. Canned peaches and cold storage apples from the root cellar were baked into pies. Pancakes were smothered in apple butter. Wild berries were boiled into preserves: blueberry, elderberry, raspberry.

Afternoons Clara sewed, mended worn clothes, created new. Lily took long walks. She carried a wicker trapper basket on her back. A water jar, some jerky, a shawl, a sheathed hunting knife and one of Edward's pistols were its contents. She also carried the twenty gauge for squirrel, rabbit, grouse or whatever came within range.

Her wanderings took her further and further back into the mountains. She followed the ridge above Bear Creek north to the head of Fisk Hollow. She climbed the steep sides of Bradley and Wokeley Hollows. Some days she hiked west into Annin township to explore the upper Two Mile and Lillibridge Creeks. She loved the solitary white pines towering above the forest with widespread branches like floating green clouds hovering above the white woods. She loved the leafless oaks, maples, ash and birch, which appeared like pen and ink drawings on paper the color of clear sky.

She learned the deer runs. They became her trails. She knew where the black bears slept and would return to those isolated dens in late winter to see the cubs. She knew where the owls nested in thick fir trees along the creek banks.

Lily witnessed the drama of the wild, the energy of yearling coyotes running with the pack, the blood of the squirrel spilled on the snow where its tracks ended in a fan of wing prints. She saw the beauty of snow banks sculpted by wind, creek ice engraved with crystal images of fern awash in the cold light of early morning, fresh tracks of field mice like a string of equal signs stamped in the snow along a fallen branch leading to a hole the size of an eye at the base of a dead beech tree.

As Lily moved through the forest, the wind spoke to her. As they slid over rock and log, the steaming springs talked. Birds whispered. She spoke to herself, long, calm assurances about good and evil, balance, memory. Having led a life of survival, she was not good at making plans, looking ahead. But, Lily thought to herself, I feel comfortable here, there is so much to learn, to see, to understand, to feel. These are real days, no dream, no nightmare. What is is. Loss, gain, beauty, danger, peace, upheaval, life.

―――――――

Early one morning after having slept in a small cave on a flat peak above Weimer's Hollow, Lily followed a game trail that headed further north. The midnight snow meant fresh tracks. Deer and coyote had already used the trail earlier that morning. Lily examined broken branches and bushes that had been nibbled. Near a thick stand of mountain laurel, she dug in the snow at the base of a birch and discovered that mice, shrews, or voles had girdled its bark. In winter, she thought, they work under snow in these elaborate tunnel systems that allow them to ignore the upper world. Lily had seen before where odor or noise had given them away, but if the snow was deep enough, she concluded, they were safe.

She marveled at the intricate lives of animals and plants. The brilliant velvet green of moss on a gray boulder in midwinter. Lichen's pale green formations looked like skin peeling from rock.

Except where it drifted across the trail, the snow was not deep. Lily moved easily among the trees, the rock fields, across the frozen marshland, beneath the gray sky. She was working her way up one side of a swale, thinking about the way animals live in the present and how healthy it would be if she could learn to do that, when she crossed a new trail running east which contained one set of human tracks. Lily froze. She listened and watched. She removed Edward's pistol from the wicker pack and placed it in the holster Clara had made which hung from her leather waist belt. The tracks, she thought, were very fresh. The sides had not collapsed nor had the sun had any effect on their precise composition. The tracks had been made by a large man. They were long and deep.

A hunter, Lily thought. A trapper. A fugitive. Papa.

She had, in all her wanderings, never encountered a soul on the trails she traveled. Often she thought she heard voices, but it was just the wind or an old conversation surfacing from the waves of her memory. Once she was certain that she saw a little girl scrambling among the rocks, but when she scrutinized the area, the snow had not been disturbed. Since, she came to think of that girl as her own self. Clara had said, Lily remembered, if you roam the woods long enough, it will accept you and reveal some of its mystery, its spirit.

But these tracks were not made by a spirit. A man made them. She followed like a stalking cat.

The tracks led along a frozen creek bed, through a stand of fir and up a steep slope littered with boulders strewn there during the last ice age. She followed the long ridge above to a clearing surrounded by oaks, maples and pines.

She heard the man speak before she saw him. Lily pressed herself against a pine and listened. Her heart raced at first because she expected to hear her father's voice. But it wasn't his. She remembered the tracks were sure footed, no dragging.

The man said, "If this world were not as it is, we would be friends. Maybe we will have to remake the world into one fit for us both. I will unburden my heart to you, tell all the stories I have lived and those told to me. When you return, you will speak of your travels, what you've seen and heard and about the great smells that live in the wildflowers far off beyond my vision."

Lily shifted and looked with one eye into the clearing. The man stood on a flat rock near the center of the snowfield. A small fire smoked near him. He wore a red wool coat and deer hide pants tucked into homemade boots. He was neither old nor young, Lily thought, Clara's age maybe. As she listened Lily thought to herself, another lunatic who talks to people who aren't there.

"I think, my friend, someone is listening to our prayer, another traveler. Hey, traveler," he called out to Lily, "I see your breath behind that tree. Come here!"

He waved her in.

"Who are you talking to, mister?"

"You, my traveling friend."

"I mean before you were talking to me."

"Oh, hawk, of course."

He raised his right arm. The red tail perched there flapped his wings several times and then settled down. The bird was wearing a leather hood. It hunched its broad, pine brown shoulders, shifted from side to side on yellow legs with talons buried in the wool of the man's coat and flashed his rust colored tail feathers. From under the monk's hood, its curved beak protruded.

Lily approached cautiously. As she drew near, she could see the red leather of the man's round face, the broken nose askew to the right, half lidded brown eyes, a smiling mouth.

"How long've you been trackin' me, missy?"

"Less than a mile, I think."

"I've seen you around. Several times, in fact. Over to Finn Hollow on Annin Crick, up Dolly Brook off Twomile, camped near Hobson on the lower Sartwell. You most often seem in deep thought, a meditation. So I don't intrude."

"Like I Did?"

"Oh, no. Your visit is welcome. Brush the snow away and sit by the fire. I'll let you hold the hawk while I tell you his story."

Once seated, Lily held up her arm. The man transferred the bird to her. She was surprised by the weight of the hawk. She had always thought they must be light as air to soar around the sky all day. The sheen of the overlapping feathers was a rich matte brown. Each feather a wonder of stiff hairs. She could feel the needle tips of the talons just touching her skin through her coat. The hood covered the hawk's eyes.

"Name's Galen Doyle. Yours might be?" the man said extending his hand which Lily shook.

"Lily."

"I thought as much. Yer livin' with Clara over on Bear Creek."

"Yes, but how'd you know?"

"I move around a bit. Talk some with people, not just hawks. So I have a general idea of things, but it don't interest me much. I'd just as soon talk with this hawk as any farmer in these valleys."

"Are you from Doyle Hollow over near Twomile?"

"They's a whole clan of us over there. Dozens of Doyles. You bet. Once in a old moon one of 'em escapes and makes a name fer hisself, but not often. We generlly like keepin' to areselves, and like the world to keep to its self. But I got me trap lines all over the place, up all these cricks and hollas. Do a good business in furs and meat. Ya gotta be on these traps every day or so. Don't want the critters to suffer too long. The big jaw traps kill good, but the little leg holds are messy. I've known foxes to ring off. They get their foot caught good, and to get away, they chew right through their own leg. More often than not, they die of infection or not being able to hunt. But some of 'em recover from the most awful wounds.

"Take hawk here. I still can't figure out how he done it, but he got his leg caught in one of my traps. They's fly fishermen on the Allegheny what'll pay real money for a bird like this. But birds, especially these hunter birds, is my spirit animal. Each of us Doyles was given a spirit animal by our Gramma Doyle. She always said she was part Indian, but they ain't no proof of it. So mine was buteos. Of course, it's all fairytales and make believe, but darned if it hasn't helped me outta some lonely places.

"I have me a younger brother, William. Gramma give him wolf as his spirit animal. He said, fat lotta good it does me with no wolf near a thousand mile. So Uncle Ben Doyle drove the farm truck clear to Canada, bought from a Inuit a sure enough wolf pup, black as shadows on a moonless night, smuggled it across the border and give it to William to raise up which he did. You wouldn't see him nowheres what he didn't have that wolf with him.

"William was eighteen when that animal was full growd. Brother decided to return him to the wild like I'm doing with Hawk here. Gramma warned him no. Said the wolf was too humanized. Wouldn't survive. But he took him back anyways where he was got from up there in Canada, let him go and drove home cryin' the whole way. A month later while he was fixin' the tractor on the hillside of the wheat field, he heard a whimperin' in the brush. William took a look see and curled up there with his feet all bloody and his coat snagged with burrs was that wolf. I tell you, it changed that boy's life.

"So I can't sell a hawk or kill one. I doctored this'n. He had a sure enough broke leg so I splintered it good and kept 'im in a small cage sos he couldn't flap around, hurt hisself. I had to hunt for him. Trapped mice, rabbits, woodchucks back in the summer. Then I built a bigger cage so he could strengthen up his wings. Hawk's been healing for near eight months. I never broke nothin', so I didn't know it took so long to mend."

Galen sat next to Lily and removed the leather hood from the raptor. Hawk flapped his wings, shook his head and went still. Hawk's breath hung white in the still air. Lily stared at the bird's eyes. The yellow-brown bursts of light deep in the pupils told stories of intense living, long flights in stormy skies, gliding descents into rock fields over a rushing earth, close calls on twilight hunts and long hungry nights spent on empty nests.

"Why didn't you give the hawk a name?" Lily said.

"You don't name wild things," said Galen. "They don't pay no mind to names. A crick was a crick long before we came along and gave it a name. Same with the rocks and trees, birds and animals. Deer don't even know they're deer. They just know they *are*. Names don't help 'em none. They only help us keep things straight, maybe makes things more personal to us. I've a feelin' animals and birds do likewise, but on a different level, more to do with smell and sound. They's as much individuals as we are.

"I seen a coyote grieve once for her dead mate just like we would. That's what that coyote done; for seven days it came back to its dead mate and lay right on top of him and whimpered all the long day. On the eighth day the body was gone. She come back and just sit there, then she went away.

"You hungry, missy? I got jerky and water," Galen said.

"Oh, no thanks. I've had plenty already this morning."

"You mind if hawk eats a little before he takes off?"

"No. Do you think I could feed him?"

"Sure. Here you go."

Galen pulled several dead mice from his coat pocket and handed the brown bodies to Lily.

"It's best to hold them by the tail when you offer them to hawk. That way he's less likely to think your finger is food."

Lily held up a mouse, which dangled like a brown pendulum before the hawk's eyes. The bird's strike startled Lily. The mouse was consumed whole in several jerky swallows. Before the final gulp, the hawk paused expressionless with the small whip of the mouse's tail protruding from its beak.

"Nothing like a tasty mouse," said Galen.

"For some reason, it doesn't make me hungry," said Lily.

"Well, a lot of animals likes 'em. There must be something to it. You ever had rattlesnake?"

"No."

"What you do is get yourself a big one and skin it out. Quarter it up and impale each piece on a thick, green stick. Prop those sticks so's the snake is cookin' over an open fire. After just a little while, brush on a little sauce you make by crushing up some tomatoes, onions or better yet scallions or even leaks if you can get 'em, a bit of mustard, a handful of garlic, of course, and whatever herbs you got drying in the kitchen. If yer cookin' a few snakes out here like where we are, forget the sauce. You can always find wild onion, mushrooms and greens for a salad. Makes a great meal. I think snakes is so good tastin' because of all the mice and toads they eat."

Lily grimaced. Galen placed a few small branches on the fire. The hawk watched blue smoke rise like a pillar into the silver sky.

Lily said, "I've never had snake, but I like venison and bear."

"Don't ever let uncle Jason hear you say that. Bears is his animal. He was the worst case of all the Doyles so far. He got to runnin' with a rough bunch from town. Out all night drinkin' whiskey, caterwaulin', drivin' the back roads, shootin' off guns drunk outta their minds. The Hackett boy from over to Smethport had an old Ford they used. Uncle Jason was pretty liquored up one night when they drove off the road 'cause of a bear asleep on a curve. They said it looked just like a pile a' coal fell off a truck. The bunch of 'em climbed out the windows of the tipped over Ford and went after that bear, which had hightailed it, up the hillside. It was near to two in the a. m. All of 'em got cut by the pricker bushes, and Hackett broke his arm runnin' smack into a tree. Gramma said it's a wonder nobody got shot.

"One thing Uncle Jason could do better than any was track. Drunk or sober there wasn't anything he couldn't follow. Light or dark, didn't matter. He listened and sniffed and followed snapped twigs before he caught up with her. He had stopped twice to be sick, but once he locks on a trail, he don't give up.

"He got that black bear up agin some rocks where, bein' cornered, she turned on him. Soon as she raised up on her hind legs, he brought up his daddy's doublebarrel twelve gauge and fired one pumpkin ball into the chest of that bear.

"When Jason tells the story, he says that the instant he pulled the trigger, he seen how low he'd sunk. Here he was shootin' his own spirit animal. Hell and damnation was too good for him he'd say. He heard that bear womp the ground like a felled tree. Most take a lifetime to change; for Uncle Jason it took about a minute. He built up a fire. The bear was unconscious but not dead. He dug the bullet out of the bear's chest and packed the hole with a poultice made of mud and pinesap. Then he smoked the wound.

"He sat with that animal for near two weeks before it regained itself enough to amble off. Gramma was the one that found him and brought food. But Uncle Jason fed it all to the bear. Said he was fasting to clear all his sins away. He stayed close to home after that. Tryin' to make up for all the trouble and anxiety he caused the family.

"What happened to the bear?" Lily asked.

"She recovered. Had a pair of cubs the following spring. I think the need to stay livin' is stronger in some creatures than others. That bear had the need. People are that way, too. Some's delicate and weak, afraid of livin'; others strong as a bear out lookin' for life, not waitin' around for it to show up."

"I think you're right," Lily said. "I've known people who were weak, and lately I've met some who are very strong."

Galen said, "I'd say that yer one of those strong ones else you wouldn't be out here in the middle of winter. You'd be home by the fire curled up in a safe nest of quilts. Also, I think it's time, missy, to give hawk here his freedom."

Galen urged the red-tail onto his arm. He stood. Lily stood and watched.

Looking into the eyes of the hawk Galen said, "Hawk, wherever you soar over these old mountains remember to check up on me. If you have power to make my way smooth rather than a path full of knotted roots, please do. Be wary of traps. Hunt well, hawk, live long and free."

With that Galen raised his arm quickly. The hawk released his grip, flapped wildly for a little altitude and glided across the snowfield to a pine branch at the edge of the forest. He landed facing away from the two standing by the fire.

After a long moment, the hawk took flight and disappeared down the misty ridge like a vanishing apparition.

Lily turned to go.

"One more minute," Galen said. "What is your animal? Who looks over you?"

"I have only Clara," she said.

"She is probably enough, but it is best to have one from the natural world, too. You know, a second species. Because I understand these things, I will give you coyote. He is the great survivor, clever in all things. No matter how many times he is killed, he will continue to make tracks in the snow. He has the gift of seeing into the hearts of others to know what is writ there. Coyote will visit you in dreams and waking, and speak to you in the silent way of spirits. Some of your thoughts will be his. When fear or confusion comes upon you, coyote will show you the way. On your way back to Bear Creek, you will see a coyote. Look into his eyes and you will know that all I have said is true. Pleasant journey, missy."

Galen hushed the fire with scoops of snow. He walked off toward the misty woods where the hawk had flown. Lily watched him go then turned toward Bear Creek.

December passed. January slipped by. February was already waning. Clara had become accustomed to Lily's absences. There were times when she'd be gone over night and sometimes several nights. Clara told Saul that even though she worried, Lily always returned in good spirits and the two of them would tell each other stories late into the night. They took turns reading aloud from Edward's books, reading poems or nature essays, or even Edward's own tales of growing up in the mountains. Tales of stormy nights, large cats and old black bears, wolves and being lost in a moonlit valley, survival accounts of eating ants, worms and slugs, long descriptions of magnificent beauty, light on water, trees, rock, and night skies scratched by meteors.

A long journal entry was about a coyote that followed Edward for days through the woods. It appeared to be watching him or watching over him. Often he'd see its tracks first then on down the trail the coyote would be waiting for him. As he approached it, it made faint whining sounds as it moved further off into the woods, its fur full of soft light, head and tail erect but not aggressive.

"Sound familiar?" Clara asked.

Lily said, "Yes. Did Edward know Galen?"

"Some, but I knew him better. He never sent some critter to guard me though."

"Galen thinks you're strong enough to take care of yourself. In fact, I bet he's even thought of sending you to watch over someone else, like me."

"Hmmm," Clara mumbled.

It was almost dark when Lily tramped down Bear Creek returning from one of her hikes. The sky was slate; the path through the old white snow was trampled dark by deer. The trees were silent shadows. The birds were still. The trail dipped and rose over a knoll just before descending past Edward's dam to the cabin. With the leaves off, from this vantage point a swath of the main road could be seen. Lily saw a dark thing move along that piece of road and disappear.

She made her way to the cabin where the dogs greeted her with barks and howls. Clara came out.

"Get the big gun! There's a bear down on the road!" Lily said. "He'll pay for leaving the den early. We'll eat good all spring."

Lily was beaming.

Clara re-entered the cabin and emerged with the 30/40 Craig rifle.

"Let's go," she said. "Lily, you lead. Stay, Curly! Spike, you stay!" The dogs set to whining.

"Hush up!" Lily said. "You scare that bear off and we'll have to eat dog this spring!" They quieted down.

Clara followed Lily. The two headed through the woods above the white garden plot in order to keep cover. Snow crunched beneath their boots. Lily's wheat colored hair lay in snarls against her back. Clara wore a knit cap, a sweater and an old pair of Edward's wool pants. They did not speak until they got to the rock outcropping that gave them a clear view of Sartwell Creek and the paved road that followed its banks.

"There! There he is!" whispered Lily pointing the direction. "You see him by that big pine?"

Clara whispered, "Oh, yes."

She raised the rifle and peered along the open sights. "Two hundred plus yards," she said softly. "It's standing on its hind legs."

The black hulk of the bear did not move. Clara raised the bead several inches and pulled the trigger. The explosion echoed around the valley. A small branch on the pine snapped and hung limp.

"Damn!" said Clara ejecting the spent shell. She leveled the rifle in the direction of the fleeing animal when Lily put her hand on Clara's.

"Wait. It's a man."

"What? Are you sure?"

"Yes, he's still upright, running, hobbling. See how he's dragging that leg."

"Did I hit him?"

"No, you hit the tree. I can't tell for sure from here, but I think that animal is Papa."

7

Darkness settled over the cabin like a thick dust. The kerosene lamps were lit. The fire in the woodstove was built up. It crackled and snapped in the great silence. Outside, the dogs were huddled in the snow asleep. A Great Horned Owl hooted from its nest in the pine above the frozen pond.

Lily was curled up in a postcard quilt on a chair in front of the open door of the woodstove. Yellow light danced around her face. Below the appearance of serenity, her mind raced. Images shouted themselves at her. Plans were born and then abandoned. Feelings boiled as she watched the yellow-blue flames flicker above the oak logs.

Clara talked aloud to Edward unsure of what to do. Lily Listened.

You remember that hideout we had, Edward, just in case something happened and we had to make a run for it? I always thought that was another one of your fictional lives out of control.

Lily continued to watch the fire, her face calm but serious. The shelves against the wall behind her bowed down in the center with the weight of Edward's books and journals. Bookmarks protruded from the tops of some. The lamplight illuminated the carved birds and animals. The firelight made them appear as if they were moving, restless. Wood feathers twitched, wood fur and scales rose and fell as if the snake and bobcat were breathing. As she did every night, Lily held the carved kestrel, Clara's gift, under the quilt, tracing its delicate features with her fingers. Clara sat next to Lily and spoke directly to her.

"Edward and I had this secret place. It was a ghost town, used to be a lumber camp back at the turn of the century I think. It was called Mina. An actual town with a school, a church, post office and a railroad. There was even a bunch of houses. Nothing fancy, just clapboard houses where the men who ran the sawmill lived with their families. The streets had names and everything. Edward's father was born there in 1911. That's how we come to be interested in it.

"Anyway, when all the trees were cut down, it was abandoned. That was years and years ago. Most of the buildings were torn down sos the area could be used as a farm. Some of the lumber was used in Coudy to build other houses. Some of the buildings that were left up Elm Flat fell to ruin. Windows gone, floors caved in, roofs collapsed, walls fallen over, trees growing up through floors, dust, dirt everywhere, scattered clothing, broken beds, canned food still on the shelves. Vandals took most of the siding so what you see is studs holding up plank walls. Everything was weathered gray. All the outhouses were tipped over, covered with vines. The place was alive with rats, snakes, spiders and bees. Animal droppings everywhere.

"I haven't been there in more than ten years, since Edward died, but he had this idea that we should have a secret place to go to just in case something happened. Once a year we'd borrow horses from Wilson, the farmer up the road, and head for Mina upriver toward Coudy. We'd follow the Allegheny the whole way right through Roulette, past Knowlton and Reed Run to Mina. A dirt road runs south of the river through Elm Flat. Back in there is what's left of the ghost town. Kids have been forbiddin in there ever since the Emerson boy got himself bit in the face by a rattler. The next day he was dead. But if you're careful like we were and make a lot of noise going in, all those critters scurry away. If you leave them be, they won't harm you. Kids just can't leave things be.

"All together I think we made five trips there. We stashed stuff in the blacksmith's shop. It was the building that seemed least likely to fall down. Edward built a strongbox way in back in one of the stalls. Each year we added to the supplies: jars of water, tins of flour, sugar, coffee, canned vegetables and fruit, an ax, a pistol and cartridges, knives, a sealed jar of kitchen matches. The last year we were there Edward left pencils and a tablet just in case we wanted to keep a diary about hiding out, one that people might find years later next to our bones, I suppose. He was always imagining such stuff. He called it *playing*.

"Well, like I said, I haven't been there in a long spell and maybe the forest has reclaimed the whole thing. It's easy enough to find though because there's a broken white pine where you turn away from the river. Just the trunk is standing. Lightening struck it. If you like, Lily, we could head up there tomorrow and wait for things to quiet down here. I could let Marsha know and your Uncle Al could drive into to town and tell the judge. It would probably only be for a few days. By then they'd have him locked up. Whada ya say, should we make a run for it?"

Lily looked at Clara. Her eyes were wet, firelight moved in them. She sighed heavily.

"Clara, I don't want to make trouble for you here. You've been so good. I should handle this myself. Even if they put him in jail, eventually they have to let him out."

"Your father, Lily, thinks he owns you. What we know is that he is a violent man. If you and I confront him now, there can only be trouble. I think we should give the law a chance to deal with him, but if it comes down to a confrontation, the two of us will just have to handle it. You see, you aren't alone any more. We're friends, you and I, and whatever happens to you, happens to me. That's the way it is."

"Okay," she relented. "I'll do whatever you say."

Before she fell asleep that night, Clara told Edward that his hideout was finally going to get some use. She said she hoped it would still be in tact and that she'd take the machete to dig through the snow and hack back the tangled growth if need be.

At first light, Clara awoke to a profound silence. The cabin was cold. Her breath hung in the air above her. She felt disappointed in herself that she had forgotten to reload the woodstove before turning in. Through the window, Clara could see that it was snowing.

She opened the door slightly to check on Lily asleep on the cot in the kitchen. The cot was empty. Clara entered the room calling, "Lily! Lily! Lily!"

There was no answer. On her pillow lay the black and white photograph of Celie. Clara picked it up and said aloud, *Edward, this is not good.*

On the back of the photograph, Lily had scribbled a note in pencil:

Clara,
I can feel him near us.

I don't want trouble for you.
It's me he wants.
I'll wait in Mina 'til he's gone.
                              Love, Lily

Clara clutched the photograph to her then dropped it on the cot. *Okay, Edward, this is what I'll do. I must tell Marsha so I'll hike over there. Then Al can bring me back here in the truck before he goes to town for the judge or he may know someone with a phone. I'll get all my gear and some extra supplies and head for Mina. With this snow, I wont make it before nightfall, but I will make it.*

Clara dressed and packed her rucksack: a water jar, a few biscuits, one of Edward's pistols and a box of shells. The other box of shells and pistol were missing. *Lily has them,* Clara thought. *Good.*

She went to the shed, cut a few strips of venison from the haunch that hung there and threw them to the dogs. Curly and Spike growled at each other momentarily and then ate as if it were their last supper.

Snow was falling harder now. Clara passed Edward's pond and headed up Bear Creek along the white path that led over the hill to Fishing Creek and Marsha's farm.

Lily crouched behind a maple trunk at the edge of the field that sloped down to the main road on the other side of which flowed the Allegheny. She peered through the heavy snowfall at the empty highway. She had hoped to make this Burtville crossing before daylight.

On the far side of the bridge, an old structure with an arched framework of iron bracing, was the Larkin farm that Clara had told her about. One of the kids Clara had saved still ran the farm. She could just make out that the barn door was open. Lily didn't want to be seen by anyone. She waited. The snow fell, the wind intensified. Icy flakes stung her cheeks. She ignored them.

Shortly, someone exited the barn and entered the house. No trucks or cars had passed on the highway. Lily moved cautiously down the field toward the road listening for the engine groan of approaching vehicles. She had crossed the road and was approaching the bridge when she heard a tractor start up. Young Larkin was getting ready to plow the drive with the faded red International Harvester, the same one that had plowed his father under.

Lily slid part way down the bank holding onto a girder. She was able to clasp a tension cable, slide under the bridge and hang there. Her deerskin mittens were bunched at the knuckles. Beneath her, the steep bank was bare earth for several feet where it ended in fast open water.

The tractor strained with individual explosions between which it seemed the engine might die. Lily looked up at the oak planks that formed the roadbed. They shuddered and clapped as the tractor moved across the bridge. She could hear the avalanche of plowed snow smack the water. A shower of dirt and snow fell upon her as the tractor passed overhead forcing grit between the planks. The noise was thunder. Lily almost lost her grip, almost cried out.

She was certain that Larkin would come back as soon as he got to the highway just fifty yards off, but he did not. The chug of the engine faded downstream until it was lost. In the silence, Lily became aware of the Allegheny moving out of ice and back into ice, a fine tinkling like crystal chimes in a slight breeze as well as the sound of deeper water flowing over rock like milk being poured into a glass that can't be filled.

Lily moved slowly out from under the bridge. Once on the road, she crossed to the other side of the river, climbed the snow wall created by the plow and slid down to the upstream pasture. She set her wicker pack on the other side of the barbed wire fence and slid under the bottom wire. Once the pack was securely on her back, she ran for the cover of the hedgerow that bordered the river. Her boots broke through the crust several times, but she kept going feeling a slight panic at the prospect of being found out, spotted from the farmhouse, seen from the barn beside which a dozen cows crowded together next to a pile of fresh mulch.

No one saw her. She followed the hedgerow to the end of the pasture, negotiated another fence and did not stop until the fields ended and the woods began. Finally, she slumped against a tree and looked back. The farm had disappeared, the bridge was gone, the fields were swallowed in a snow thick as fog. Everything was so silent except for Lily's heartbeat, her heavy breathing and the snow fine as sugar hitting dead leaves still clinging to pin oaks and hickory.

Lily sat for a long time. Eventually she removed her pack and took long swallows from a jar of water. Out of habit, she reached into her pocket just to feel the reassurance of her mother's picture. "Damn," she said. "I should've used something else."

Shouldering her pack, Lily continued on keeping the river in view or at least within earshot. She loved the watery voices of the Allegheny, the whispers, the laughter, the excited talk of the rapids, even the hushed movement of water under ice that formed over deeper pools. It was those pools that made her think of Celie. Mother was like that, she thought to herself, calm on the surface, an unchanging face turned to the world, but so much emotion moving under her pale skin. Lily thought, I wonder if she was ever happy. Does sorrow drown joy or is joy a rock over which sorrow flows?

The snow rained down heavy and fine. The only map she had was in her head, Clara's words. She repeated them over and over again. There was no path to follow. Lily proceeded along deer trails, a way of traveling with which she was familiar.

She felt strangely happy out in this storm, dependent only on herself in a landscape she understood. She did not succumb to the dark clouds of memory that pursued her. When they seemed about to overtake her on the trail, Lily would whirl around and face them as if they were actual enemies, visible foes. "Stop right there!" she would yell into the falling snow. "Don't you dare come any closer! You'll not be the boss of me anymore; you don't rule me; you have no control now! I have it!"

Then Lily would spin around, keep marching and say out loud to herself, "Christ, I'm as bad as Clara talking to Edward all the time. There, I'm doing it again."

As the morning wore on, the storm eased, the snow abated and visibility improved. By noon Lily was approaching Roulette, a tiny village along the river. There was no woods to hide in, no hedgerows in which to conceal one's self. Lily trudged slowly along the bank through foot deep snow. She could hear voices, children playing in the snow on a knoll near a white clapboard house. An old woman was hanging clothes on a line. A boy was shoveling a walk. The old woman called out to her. Lily waved, but did not answer. She picked up her unsteady pace.

Near the far side of town was a log cabin close to the river's bank. Dead cars and rusted farm machines were scattered about the yard. An empty bird feeder hung from a willow tree whose leafless branches drooped to the white ground. Blue wood smoke curled out of the stone fireplace the top of which was stained with creosote the color of tobacco spittle. A shed behind the house listed toward the river as if it were about to topple. Long red underwear and wool socks hung frozen on a line strung from the willow to the shed. The clutter was made soft by the new fallen snow.

Lily hesitated for a moment trying to figure a safe way around the place. She heard the chain rattle just before the black dog lunged, growling at her. Her heart clenched as she fell backward. The mongrel was jerked to a stop by the chain, but it remained at arm's length snarling and leaping against his tether. Lily scooted back away from the animal. A screen door banged shut.

"Shut the hell up, you goddamn dog!" a man yelled from the yard. The dog quieted and slunk back to its plywood shelter. The man was dressed in wool pants held up by black suspenders that hung over soiled, red long underwear. He called out through a thick gray beard, "Who's there? What are you doing here?"

Lily's voice cracked. "It's just me. I don't mean no harm, mister. I was just out for a hike and didn't see the dog. Sorry."

The man approached.

"You sure picked a hell of a day to be about. Don't pay no mind to Old Sally here. She's goin' on fourteen, half deaf, most of her teeth's gone. She don't see so good either. Named her after a girlfriend a mine that got all those same qualities. It's a wonder all this excitement didn't do 'er in. Where you from, girl?"

The man's eyes were the color of rock moss. A few snowflakes fell on his bald head, landed in the nest of his beard. He took Lily's mittened hand and helped her to her feet.

"Up Sartwell Creek," Lily answered brushing snow from her legs. She pulled her knit cap down over her ears.

"Your people know you're trekking about in snow like this?"

"Oh, yes! I do it all the time. Thanks, mister. I'll just be on my way."

"What way is that? You have any idea where yer goin' to?"

"Usually I don't, but today I'm just following the river to see what there is to be seen. Nice day, don't you think?"

"Nice day!? Why yer crazier than me! All the way here from Sartwell, on foot, in a storm! You plannin' on going all the way to Coudy?"

"No, sir. Don't like towns much. I'll turn back before then and cut over the mountains. That way I won't upset your dog on my return."

"Yer a piece of work, little miss. I wouldn'ta figured a growd man to be taken on this kinda hardship, let alone some woman."

"Well, I'm just a girl, sir. I better be running along. Nice talking to you."

Lily turned to go.

"Hold on there. Name's Ephraim. If ya run outta daylight, I want you to come stay here. I got room and it wouldn't be no bother. You could be on yer way first light."

"Thank you, sir, but the best part of being out is the night time."

Lily smiled and headed upstream.

Ephraim turned to Old Sally. "Don't that just beat all. If I had me a dollar bill, Old Sal, I'd bet we was going to have some company tonight. What do you think of that?"

The dog whined.

Clara paced back and forth in Marsha's kitchen studying first the crucifix above the door to the living room then the window that looked out on the side yard. Marsha, wearing a yellow apron, gray hair tied with a blue bandanna, was standing by the enameled metal table tenderizing a large slab of beef by pounding it with the edge of a thick ceramic dessert plate. Each strike was amplified by the reverberation of the metal table, an incessant banging on a drum. Outside the kids screamed their joy throwing snowballs, sliding down a slight slope on cardboard squares and rolling snow for snowmen. The youngest, Arlin, sat on the porch steps and cried near hysterics.

Clara finally said, "I really admire how you handle all this, this noise."

"It's tribal livin', dear," said Marsha. "If Al had taken this cow last year, I might not have to bang away at it so much. As for these kids, they have a lotta energy. Arlin there just wants attention from the others, from me. When he don't get it, he'll try somethin' else. Hopefully, it'll be a quieter approach. They do keep me goin'. Why don't you sit down and have some tea. Al won't be long, the snow's lettin' up and soon enough you'll be on yer way. No use frettin' over what you can't do nothin' about. That Lily's got a mind of her own. She can take care of herself. Ya know, she's a lot like you, Clara."

Clara looked at Marsha. "You think so?"

"I know so. You don't like people helpin' ya, but you'd do anything for those that ask. Lily, she's just trying to protect you. She figures if Orin don't find her at your place, he'll leave you be."

Clara watched the snow fall in the barnyard. "I think she's taken on more than she can handle. This so-called father of hers is a dangerous man. I just can't stop thinking about her. Out there in this storm searching for a place she's never been to before."

Marsha ceased her pounding, wrapped the meat in wax paper and placed it in the icebox.

"Listen, Clara," she said, "the gunshot yesterday probably scared the bejesus outta that old man, and he's headed back to where ever he come from. Besides, you taught Lily good. Let the law handle it like you said. Here comes Al now. If he seems nervous, it's not Orin he's worried about. It's this blamed snow. The roads ain't been plowed and that old Ford truck just ain't trustworthy."

"You ready yet, Clara?" said Al stomping snow off his boots. His broad smile belied the mischievous greeting. He removed his gloves, pulled out a small paper square and sack, opened the sack with one hand, tapped tobacco onto the paper, balanced it while pulling the sack ties to with one hand and clenched teeth, returned the sack to his wool shirt pocket, rolled the paper into a lumpy cylinder, licked the edge with spittle to secure it and stuck the cigarette in his smiling mouth. Marsha struck a kitchen match and held it up. Al puffed then blew out a circle of smoke that drifted a moment before dissipating.

"Ready? I've been pacing here near an hour. What took you so long?"

"Dang Ford wouldn't turn over. Had to go out to the field and get the battry offen the tractor and put it in the truck. Then I had to chain up. But don't you worry. We'll stop at your place so's you can get those provisions you want. Then to town to see the judge. I bet we have you up to Mina even before Lily gets there. We got us over a foot a snow out there, so we best get along."

Like the Fishing Creek road, Sartwell had not been plowed. Al moved slowly along the untrodden white path. It was nearly noon when they neared the gravel drive that led up Bear Creek. What had appeared to Clara from a distance to be mist hanging in the valley she knew now to be smoke.

The source at first was difficult to determine. Then Clara said touching Al's shoulder, "Al, this is not good. It's coming from my place."

Al turned up toward the cabin, maneuvered the truck past the garden plot and into the yard. Clara just stared as they sat in the idling truck.

Flames poured out of the front door, out the side window, up through the stone chimney. Black and gray smoke rose in a twisted column a hundred feet before flowing down the hollow. The sound of breaking glass could be heard. Clapboards curled like black lips and turned to ash. Two front windows, charred black, looked like empty eye sockets. A rush of air being sucked skyward sounded like a howling storm, a tortured scream.

"Oh, my god," whispered Clara.

Al opened his door first. The intense heat caused him to close it and roll the truck back fifty feet. Both got out of the truck.

"You got buckets?" Al yelled.

"Yes, in the shed," Clara shouted. "But it's no use, the pond's frozen. Forget it, Al, we're too late. I don't understand it. The stove was out cold when I left this morning."

The roof gave way, booming and cracking as it collapsed through the cabin. Sparks, ash and smoke blew out in a dark rushing cloud. Clara went down on her knees and stared. The orange light colored her face, her hunched figure.

How could this happen? Oh, Edward, I'm so sorry. All your stories. She began to sob, tears flowed as ash fell about her. *Oh, Edward, all your books. Edward.*

Al grabbed the splitting maul and headed for the pond to crack through the ice. He looked back at Clara.

He shouted, "Hey come up here and give me..."

His voice trailed off. Sprawled on the windblown ice were Curly and Spike, a pool of blood stained the frozen surface beneath their heads.

"Oh, my lord," he said quietly to himself. Al removed his jacket and tried to cover the dogs. Boot prints lead from the dogs to the cabin and then back again disappearing up the trail along the creek.

Al went to Clara.

"Clara, there's nothing can be done now. Orin's been here. He killed both pups and torched the place."

Clara moved toward the pond.

"Don't look, Clara. He cut their throats. We gotta go for help. You've gotta pull yerself together. Damn good thing you and Lily wasn't here when he came. No tellin' what the son-bitch mighta done. We gotta go for help and find Lily."

"Okay, okay, I'm okay," Clara sniffed, wiped both eyes with her sleeve and tried to calm her breathing. "Just give me a minute."

The fire roared, crackled, snapped, spit flame and billowing smoke. Clara brushed snow from the stump, all that remained of the tree that had taken Edward from her, and sat quietly. She could not look at the burning cabin or at the pond where the dogs lay. She searched the snowy ground for answers.

"I don't think he has more 'n an hour's head start," said Al. "Maybe he's headed for my place because he don't know about Mina. We really gotta go, Clara. We can stop down to Burtville. Larkin's gotta phone. He can get the sheriff out here and we can make it back to my place. I'll come back later and see to the dogs."

Clara noticed a piece of paper in the snow exposed by a footprint. She picked it up.

"Look, Al, it's part of Celie's picture. Here's the rest of it. I left it on Lily's cot this morning. She wrote a note to me on the back. Orin must've seen it, now he knows."

8

The Allegheny River meandered through a thick woods, stretched itself out straight for half a mile, split around a pair of small islands and then curled along the base of a woodlot. At Reed Run, Lily crossed a wooden bridge. She was breathing heavily and could feel sweat roll down her back. After crossing an open field that was littered with folded cornstalks sticking out of the snow like broken bones, she rested behind a clump of tall sumac. She set the basket on a tree stump, removed her coat and folded it into the pack. She sat in the snow for a long time. Her eyes continuously scanned the landscape; her ears were alert. A few deer were foraging near the far edge of the cornfield. Chickadees fluttered among the sumac. The sky was low and gray.

Lily's thoughts were cluttered. Meeting Ephraim was a bad sign, she thought. She said to herself, I didn't want anyone but Clara to know my whereabouts. Clara must be on her way here by now. The storm is over. It won't cover my tracks anymore. I should be there soon. What was it Clara said, a broken tree? I sure hope that's still there.

Then the day old memory replayed itself. A shot rang out and the black figure of her father ran off dragging his leg. Lily tried to shut off her thinking. She stood, slid into her pack and moved upstream.

The afternoon grew old. The forest along this section of the river was thick with undergrowth. Barbed tendrils reached out from their snow cover to grab at Lily's arms, legs and face. The irregular ground beneath the snow caused her to stumble and fall. At times she crawled on hands and knees snagging her basket on the web of interlacing branches above. Snow fell in clumps onto her neck.

The animal trail Lily was following had been used recently. She found tracks with very little snow in them. She examined the paw prints and their configuration in the snow. Two forward, two back, one slightly behind the other, distinct claw marks.

"Coyote," she said aloud.

Lily looked up the trail as far as she could see, but there was no coyote there.

By the time she entered the clearing, Lily was shivering and miserable. Ahead was a snowy path that led away from the river and was wide enough to be a road. She was startled to see a farmhouse so close. The brush had been too dense for her to see very far ahead. Adjacent to the house was a large barn. The red paint had faded and chipped so that the sign on its west side was unreadable.

There, where the white road curved south, stood a massive tree trunk, barkless, riddled with woodpecker holes, weathered gray. Along the edge of the road were coyote tracks.

"That's it," Lily whispered.

———————

Al slid in behind the wheel of the old, blue Ford and pulled the door closed. The truck idled loudly. The heater fan whirred pushing air that was neither warm nor frozen. He looked at Clara.

"Larkin's on the phone already. He's calling Sheriff Tauscher and your brother-in-law Saul in town and Big Earl who lives up near my place. Earl will check on Marsha and the kids. The Sheriff and Saul will meet us at Mina. Larkin said he'd give 'em all the directions then he'd be along as soon as he gets his truck goin'. Must have the same Ford I got. He wanted us to wait on the sheriff, but I told him waiting was something you weren't good at. Told him we was ready for any kind of situation that might come up."

Clara stared out the partially frosted window. There was enough clear glass that she could see the bridge, the field and woods through which Lily must have passed early in the morning. To herself she mumbled, *Edward, this girl's in real trouble and she doesn't know it, or maybe she knows better than I do which could be why she took off like that. She's done that before.*

"What's that you say?"

"We better go, Al," she said aloud.

Al pulled on his canvas work gloves, pushed in the clutch, moved the stick to first and slowly headed toward the bridge. The truck rattled over the oak planks clattering like the tractor earlier that morning. Al eased the Ford out onto Route 6, which was still deep in snow. Roulette, normally just minutes away, was further today. The chains helped, but their grip was uncertain. Al kept it under twenty.

Clara watched the riverbanks. Lily could be anywhere. She watched the river move in and out of ice. Sometimes the calm stretches were completely frozen, covered with snow and already tracked up by deer. The exposed rapids steamed in the frigid air creating frost on the overhanging sumac and pine branches.

Clara scrutinized every fenced field, meadow, corn lot. She untangled the trees and undergrowth searching for Lily. Every dark tree stump, exposed log was a momentary heart pang. She'd clutch tighter to the pack that sat on her lap. Then as the realization came that each dark form was not Lily, she would relax her grip.

Al tried to keep a conversation going, but Clara was too intent on her own thoughts to take part.

He said, "You know, if that shot of yers had been just a bit to one side last night, we'd all be home by our fires today instead of chasing around the countryside in foul weather for a run away and her insane father. No use frettin' over what can't be changed I always say. I wish I'da brought my long gun. It's got a scope so's you really know what yer shootin'. Got my bear with it last year up Bark Shanty Hollow not too far from where we're headed. One shot. Three hundred yards!"

Clara looked at Al.

"Well, over two hundred anyway. Dressed out at four hundred ten pound. Got 'im right through the neck. Didn't harm any meat or the skin. Had to get the horse to drag 'im out. One shot. Two hundred and some yards. .30-06. Extended barrel. More of a target rifle I guess, but sure is great for huntin'."

Clara looked for Lily while Al talked on. "You remember that ten pointer I got up to Durward two years back? I believe, Clara, I gave you some of that venison 'cause it'd been a lean year for you."

She gave him a look.

"I haven't had a lean year. You just had too much even for that brood of yours. I just passed it along to Wilson up the valley. He doesn't hunt ever since his boy had that accident hunting grouse. Better watch the road there, Al."

Al jerked on the wheel, went sideways slightly and straightened out. He slowed to fifteen as they passed Roulette.

"What are these damn plows waiting for? The snow to melt? For spring?"

"They'll be along, Al. This is a good speed. I can see the river better. Maybe Lily's out there somewhere."

"I just hope that scoundrel father of hers broke through the ice and drowned hisself. That would be real justice, a drowned man returns alive and then drowns agin. Maybe this time he'll stay put, the sumbitch arsonist asshole. You know, Clara, I sure wish I knew how to swear better'n I do. There's times when it sure would come in handy."

"You stick with me and I'll teach you as best I can."

Al smiled.

No one had traveled the road since the storm hit. As they broke east of Roulette, the snow was a level foot deep except where drifts piled up to two feet across the road. Al could see the rises ahead like waves in the road. He picked up speed so that he could break through the high spots. It was near Knowlton that he lost control. The truck hit the long drift sideways and slid in slow motion off the road parking itself facing upstream in Trout Brook.

Al gripped the wheel, stared up the frozen creek and said, "Fuck."

"I think you're learning," said Clara.

Al tried low gear, tried reverse, then shut off the engine.

"Damn it all to hell! Judas Priest! I was sure we was gonna make it! Sorry, Clara."

"Sorry nothing, Al. We're almost there. We'll just have to walk. We can get the truck later after all this is sorted out. I don't think anyone's going to steal it."

"Okay. You're right. Let's climb outta here. Damn truck."

Al opened his door and stepped out onto the ice. Clara couldn't open the passenger door so she slid out Al's side. Al reached inside and got the twelve-gauge pump from the gun rack. He felt in his bib overalls for shells, pulled out three red, Remington deer slugs and loaded his gun.

"Not much good beyond a hundred yards," he said, "but if it makes contact, the message is clear. You still got that pistol?"

"Yes. It's already loaded."

The pair scrambled up the steep bank, brushed the snow from their arms and legs and continued along the road toward Mina. Al looked back a moment at the blue roof of the Ford. He instinctively checked the barrel of the shotgun to make sure no snow had jammed in the muzzle. He worked the pump action to chamber a shell and checked the safety.

As they waded through the deep snow, under a low gray sky, Al said, "Did I ever tell you about the time we was coon huntin' and Jasper Morgan's twenty gauge exploded because of mud stuck in the muzzle."

"Several times," Clara said.

"Well, you shoulda seen that barrel. The end split four ways to Sunday and curled back like black ribbon. 'Course he lost an eye over it which weren't too funny, but the surprised look on his face sure was somethin'. And then there was Moss Tooley over to Card Crick. Crossing a fence, he shot his big toe clean off, and Milton who was huntin' with us at the time said, "About time you hit somethin'.""

Clara smiled and said, "You told me that one, too."

———

Lily studied the soft line of the main road hoping to see Clara, but nobody was there. The hill beyond rose up, a great hump of snow thick with leafless trees. Crows called each other from the woods.

She turned away working her way south to the monolithic tree trunk. She touched it with her hand as if it could give comfort. Lily continued shuffling through the white powder replaying in her head Clara's description of Mina. All those people, she thought, living, working, fearing, loving, remembering. Every one gone. No trace.

Lily imagined voices of men calling from lumber wagons, women talking in the general store, children at recess in the schoolyard. The train whistle blast and its echo down the valley. The steam engines at the mill, the scream of the saw, the smell of sawdust and the pungent odor of the millpond like the one she had lived near in Bradford.

"I better concentrate on what's here, not what was," she said aloud.

Soon she came to a place where the road divided. The left fork of the road was more of a trail leading off through a broad flat area while the road she had been following disappeared up the hill. The coyote had gone left. Lily went left.

Now Clara told me, she thought to herself, that what little was left of this place would be up here a ways. It's going to be a hard night if nothing's left standing. Maybe I can find a windfall up in those trees.

Lily came into an area thick with bushes all humped over under the weight of snow. Beyond were four, flat square areas. They were lined up in a row. Sticking up on the far side of the last square and leaning slightly toward her was a vine-covered wall.

This is it, she thought.

Lily maneuvered around snow mounds, climbed onto the closest platform, waded several steps and broke through the floor to her waist.

"Christ, I gotta take it slow," she scolded herself.

She wriggled her way out and lay prostrate on the snow. The wicker basket dumped its contents beside her. She sat up, picked up the pistol and shells, wiped them free of snow, removed her pack and refilled it except for the water jar. She took a long drink and placed the blue glass container back in the pack.

Lily crawled off the platform and worked her way among the tall shrubs often being pelted with small avalanches of powder. A barbed shoot grabbed at her face and drew blood along the left side of her chin. Burrs stuck to her brown jacket.

Every few steps Lily looked back to make sure no one was there. She felt uneasy about the clear trail she left in the snow. Couldn't be helped, she thought. She went on past the leaning wall. Beyond was a high mound of snow out of the center of which poked a stone chimney. The fieldstones were moss green, the top a white dome. Further along there were no more platforms, no other structures, just a field humped with snow stretching up to the tree line at the base of Mina Hill.

Lily began brushing away the snow exposing a dense network of vines over upright beams. Although it was quite dark within, she could see that the floor was dirt. Using the same hunting knife she had used to field dress her deer, she cut at the tangled web creating a hole large enough for her to enter.

Lily sat in the dirt for a long time allowing her eyes to adjust to the dim light.

"Hey you bears," she called out, "you in here?"

There was no answer.

Gradually she realized that the shack she had discovered had been built on stilts and that she was under the floor in the low crawlspace. She thought of snakes living there. The floor joists above her were covered with a thin cloth spun by spiders.

Good thing it's winter, she thought, then shuddered.

Lily crawled deeper into the dark raising a fine dust. Near the base of the fireplace was a section of collapsed flooring where two joists had given way. She kicked at the planks. They snapped apart. Dim light came from above. Lily slithered up through the opening dragging her pack behind her.

She leaned against the stone wall of the fireplace hugging her pack, knees drawn up. Her breath hung in the air. Years ago half the roof had fallen flat to the floor. Above it a mesh of wild grape vines, thick as a man's arm, formed a half dome covered with snow. The vine bark, the corrugated tin roof lying on the floor and the stone against which she huddled were encased in frost. The other half of the peaked roof was sagging but still in place. Three walls remained in tact although the window casings were shuttered with vines and snow. In a corner lay a rusted kerosene lantern, its glass globe in curved pieces nearby. There was no sign of the strongbox that Edward had built.

Lily sat listening to the silence. Off somewhere deep in the woods she could hear a howl, long and melancholy, a coyote calling to someone, to her. It is the one whose tracks I saw, she thought.

"Clara should be here soon," she said aloud. "It'll be dark in a little bit. I can build a fire then."

She searched through her pack. Removed the pistol. Checked to see that it was loaded. Laid it beside her. She took out a cloth sack and the jar of water. From the sack she removed two biscuits. Lily ate with her eyes closed.

———————

"Sure wish I hadn't left my coat back at your place. It's beginning to chill down some."

"Just keep walking. You'll heat up in no time," Clara said.

"S'pose you're right. Just the same, a coat would make things more tolerable. Damn truck. Hardly worth trading in if it can't stay on the road."

"A truck is only as good as its driver."

"Yeah, well."

"Actually, even someone in a new truck would've done the same as you."

"True enough. I didn't seem to have much of a say in the matter. What is it?"

Clara had stopped in the road and held her hand up for Al to stop.

"You see that up there," she said.

She pointed toward the open field that stretched up the hillside a thousand feet to the tree line.

"What?"

"That trail coming down from the woods. Something's passed through here since the snow fell. Looks to cross the road up ahead."

"Probly just deer."

"You know well as me deer zigzag down a hill. Only a human would go straight down like that. Come on, Al."

The two moved quickly along the highway to where the tracks crossed.

"Boot tracks!" said Clara. "Look familiar?"

"Yes, but how'd he get out in front of us?"

"He must've had more of a head start than we figured. Looks to have come straight over the hills. How the hell does he even know where to go?"

"Celie told Marsha years back that Orin and his buddies used to hunt deer near Roulette. They never stopped by to visit though. So you can bet he knows right where he is."

"And where Lily is, too. We're going to run out of daylight soon."

"So's he, Clara. So's he."

Lily felt chilled in her dream. She snuggled down in her bedcovers staring wide-eyed out into her dark room. The bedroom door rattled, the handle turned.

She sat up startled, awake.

"Who's there?" she cried out into the dark space of the crumpled shack.

There was no answer, no sound. She felt the floor for the pistol, held it against her chest and waited. The cold was intense. Her whole body shivered. The darkness was everything.

After several moments she calmed herself and moved around the black space from memory. She collected broken planks from the floor, gathered dry leaves together on the flat hearth of the fireplace, pulled wall lath for kindling, stacked them on the leaves and struck a match. The leaves flared up igniting the slats. They in turn glowed under the planks she placed there. Flames grew. The cave like roof and vines vibrated in the orange light. The clogged chimney did not draw. Smoke poured out of the fireplace in a stream and pooled against the ceiling. By the fire's light, Lily was able to pull a long slat from the wall. She pushed it through the vine roof over and over creating a vent through which the smoke spewed. More planks were placed on the fire. The dry wood snapped and spit, the flames burned blue and yellow. Shadows moved along the walls.

Lily sat cross-legged absorbing the heat. She put her water jar near the flames so that the ice film that had formed would thaw. She ate another biscuit and chewed a piece of venison jerky.

Lily spoke to the fire. "Where's Clara? She should be here by now."

Lily rubbed her face with her mittened hands. The shivering had ceased. "It must be late. I'm sure the storm held her up, but it stopped hours ago. Edward, give her a message for me. Tell Clara I'm scared. I need her."

Long moments passed. The fire hissed. The world outside was hidden away from her thinking. There was only this place, this time. Her breathing eased to a regular cadence as she watched the fire. She was safe on an island floating in a wide, white sea. The rhythm of the lapping waves was in sync with the dancing flames. Sparks rose into distinct constellations before being snuffed out like eyes closing. The smoke told stories to Lily of others gathered around campfires back through the centuries. She listened intently and felt less alone, felt her strength return.

The night deepened. Sleep was settling on her when she heard movement outside. An isolated sound like a clump of snow falling on other snow. A dull thump. A footstep perhaps. A coat brushing a bush laden with snow. She did not call out. No one had called her name. She heard more. A swishing, shuffling in deep snow as if something were prowling about for a way in.

Lily whirled around to face the noise. She held the pistol up in the light and rolled the cylinder to make sure it was loaded. It was.

The dome of vines shook violently. Slush fell in large wet clumps from the ceiling. Snow was being scraped away from the vine wall. Still, nobody called her name.

Lily kneeled, leveled the pistol at the disturbance and cocked the hammer. White powder spilled onto the floor as a hole the size of a face appeared in the wall.

At first, eyes were all that Lily could see. She breathed deeply.

"Steady," she said to herself.

The eyes moved closer and peered in. Lily recognized her father's face, the deep scar on the right cheek, the dark, wild eyes, the gray-black beard. He squinted into the light.

"Lily!" he called out in his animal voice.

"Don't you come in here, Papa. Don't you."

"Nonsense, girl. You's my flesh and blood. I just come for a visit. Now put that thing down, child."

His face vanished. The first hatchet blow caused the vines to shudder. Another. Then another. They came in rapid succession unraveling the tight weave. Lily's hands shook. Her eyes grew wet. She wiped them with her sleeve.

"You can't come in here, Papa," she cried.

The hatchet continued its work. She watched as the aperture grew. Then silence. She waited. Orin reached one hand inside and pulled himself through the hole still clutching the hatchet in the other hand.

He lay on the floor for a moment looking at his daughter. The long black coat was covered with snow, his tangled hair matted with sweat. Lily could see the reflection of fire in his eyes.

"Don't, Papa," she said, her voice steadier than before. "You don't own me anymore. You gotta go!"

"What a silly little thing you are," he smiled, his teeth the color of old wood. "I just come for what's mine."

He rose to lean against the vines, his bad leg sagging.

"Now all I wants," he continued, "is for you to come along with me so's we kin be a family agin."

Orin gripped the hatchet and moved toward Lily dragging his bad leg.

———

Clara and Al flagged down the snowplow as it approached from Coudersport, its headlight beams feeling along the dark road like antennae, yellow lights sliding around the hill, the valley, the river. The driver, Jimmy Huff, turned the yellow rig around. On their way to Mina, Clara laid out the details of what had happened.

"What's the shotgun for, Al?" Jimmy asked.

"It's for a lowlife, no good varmint skunk!"

Jimmy turned south at Mina onto the Elm Flat road, crossed the narrow bridge and plowed past the tree trunk. In the headlights, two sets of tracks could be seen. Clara pulled out Edward's pistol and spun the cylinder. Jimmy's eyes widened.

"Holy shit! You two really mean business!"

"You've known me for years, Jimmy. Ever know me to hurt anyone?"

"Nope."

"So you know this is real important."

"I heard of that Lily girl in Coudy. They say she's a real nice kid who is just at home in the woods as any animal."

"It's true," said Al. "Now, Clara, you better just back me up. We don't want anyone accidentally getting hurt with that thing."

"If that's the case, you don't want me walking behind you. Jimmy, make a left here. Just follow those tracks."

"Sorry, Clara. No way I can take this thing up there. It'll get stuck for sure. Then we'll all be stuck."

"Better let us out. But don't go anywhere."

The two slid out of the truck. Al followed as Clara traced the tracks back into the brush. They were just yards along when a shot cracked the silence like a plank falling on a wood floor.

"That's Edward's pistol," said Clara.

Al undid the safety of his twelve-gauge. They hurried along the path, which was intermittently lighted by the rotating amber lights of the plow. A siren could be heard screaming along the main road.

Two more shots exploded ahead, the echo filling the flat with stuttering thunder. Clara pushed through the brush, past the leaning wall to the wrecked dome of Lily's hideout. Al helped Clara shimmy up to the opening Orin had made. He followed.

Sitting back on her heels was Lily, her eyes focused on the dark figure beside her. She still held the pistol with both hands. The hatchet was stuck in the floor next to the hearth. Blood was collecting in a pool under Orin. The fire flickered.

Clara moved quickly to the girl, removed the pistol from her hands and handed it to Al. She held onto Lily.

"I was so afraid, Lily, so afraid. It'll be okay now. It really will. Let's get out of here."

The two crawled along the floor to the hole in the vine wall and slid out. Al felt Orin's wrist, let his limp arm drop and went out. He reset the safety on his twelve-gauge. As they moved along the path, Clara held Lily. Lily did not speak. They did not need to ask what happened.

9

Celie appeared on the other side of the campfire, her face animated by the yellow flames growing among the weathered sticks. Wood smoke curled about the rock ceiling of the cave and flowed out into the dark night. The cave walls were a moonscape of craters, bumps, and hollows which looked as if they had been bombarded through the millennia by hot stones hurled by some explosion out at the edge of the universe. Curled close enough to the fire to absorb heat slept a coyote, his tawny fur rising and falling with each breath.

Lily felt a great calm and wished to reach out to her mother, but instinctively knew that that would be a violation of the dream and that Celie would vanish. Lily waited for her to speak. And she did so, but not in spoken words. She talked to Lily in a kind of animal telepathy, the secret communication that enables each individual bird in a flock to bank and turn simultaneously, the silent language wolves and coyotes speak when the pack is on the scent.

Celie told Lily that grief is both a sickness and a cure. It is a prolonged heartache that shrouds the spirit in a fog of loneliness and sorrow during which time the pearl of our hope is diminished to a dim light deep in a cave such as this. It is grief that causes the soul to become a wanderer like you, Lily, searching this forest for the lost path you once knew. But it is that same grief, Celie continued, that surrounds the seed of your hope like a shell and protects it through its protracted convalescence. Like any seed that falls on fertile soil, it will grow. Strength returns. Health is restored. Happiness becomes a possibility again.

Lily felt the heat of her mother's words, or was it the fire, cover her like a blanket. Her mind became a still pool, calm water, a mirror of trees, mountains, sky.

You are there now, Celie said to Lily. *It is time. You can let go of grief and fear. Find comfort in your wandering through the woods, find comfort in others, and give that same gift back to those you meet whose injuries are still open wounds.*

Lily looked at the dying fire. She looked back at Celie whose image was fading like a morning moon, a skin of light, then gone. The coyote awoke, rose up stretching and trotted off into the dark. The firelight left the cave. Lily listened for a while to the night sounds, and then curled up on the rock floor and slept.

www.ingramcontent.com/pod-product-compliance
Lightning Source LLC
Chambersburg PA
CBHW052147170626
46812CB00004B/1620